A HOLIDAY TO REMEMBER
A PRIDE AND PREJUDICE NOVELLA

JENNIFER REDLARCZYK

REDLARK PRESS

A Holiday to Remember ~ A Pride and Prejudice Novella

Copyright © 2018 by Jennifer Redlarczyk

Cover Art by Daniel Ichinose ~ Atomatron Designs

Interior Design by E-book Formatting Fairies

Published by Jennifer Redlarczyk ~ Redlark Press

Redlark Press

All rights reserved. Without limiting the rights under the copyright reserved above, no part of this publication may be reproduced, stored in or introduced into a retrieval system, or transmitted, in any form, or by any means (electronic, mechanical, photocopying, recording, or otherwise) without the prior written permission of both the copyright owner and the publisher of this book except in the case of brief quotation embodied in critical articles and reviews. Thank you for respecting the author's work. Jennifer Redlarczyk.

This is a work of fiction. Names, characters, places, brands, and incidents are either the product of the author's imagination, or are used fictitiously. Any resemblances to actual persons, living or dead, events, business establishments, or locales are entirely coincidental with the exception of those taken from Jane Austen's novel, *Pride and Prejudice*.

ISBN-13: 978-1983478062

ISBN-10: 1983478067

November 2018

In memory of my first choral director, Allene M. Curl, and to so many music teachers who have devoted their lives to inspiring young people by sharing their love of music, I dedicate this small offering.

ACKNOWLEDGMENTS

Being a moderator on the Private JAFF forum DarcyandLizzy.com, I wish to thank Brenda Webb, my fellow moderators and of course so many readers who have been very encouraging of my work. In addition, many thanks go out to my Beta team: Wendy Delzell, Jessica Ferree, Betty Jo Kennedy, and to Vicki Sroka who served as a cold reader. Then I would like to make mention of Melinda Reinhart and her Merrillville, Indiana High School Choirs, who were the inspiration for this story. Finally, I would also like to thank my son, Daniel Ichinose, who offered his creative talent in creating the cover design for my book and to my husband Greg who always puts up with my JAFF obsession.

Thank you all! ~ Jennifer Redlarczyk ♫

CHAPTER 1

CONNECTIONS

Meryton Academy for the Performing Arts
Monday, 4 December
Present day

"Liz Bennet! Please tell me I didn't hear what I just thought I heard!" Charlotte Lucas burst through the doors of the choir room and marched straight to the keyboard where Elizabeth was working out the final arrangements for *A Holiday to Remember*—part of the music academy's final showcase before the winter break.

"Char, I have no idea what you're talking about, and I'm kind of on a deadline here. Uh ... you do remember I have a major rehearsal at six o'clock tonight?" She arched a questioning eyebrow in her friend's direction before entering the final chords on the master lead sheet in her computer.

"Right, but for *your* information, Mr. Billy Collins just told everyone in the teacher's lounge he has a big date with *you* on New Year's Eve. He *says* he's escorting you to the Pemberley Foundation's charity gala at Forest Ridge. What gives? Don't those tickets start at five hundred a pop? Not to mention any woman who would dare to go out with that nutter would have to be a marble short."

Elizabeth stopped what she was doing and burst into laughter. "Char, do you honestly think BC would actually shell out *that* kind of money just to have a date with *me?* The man is so tight he probably wouldn't spend five dollars on his own mother. Don't worry. The Vocalteens were asked to perform at the gala and will be doing the opening act right after dessert. Since Reeves will be out of town, I'm making do with *Billy-boy* to run sound. You're welcome to join us if you don't have a date. I can always use an extra chaperone. Plus, after the kids leave, the *adults* are invited to stay and enjoy the rest of the party. There's going to be a live band, dancing, loads of food and some kind of a silent auction. It could be fun, even *without* dates."

"Sorry, Liz. As a matter of fact, *I do* have a date." Charlotte straightened up and fluttered her eyelashes in jest. "And … as much as I'd like to hobnob with the *rich and famous*, Brexton Denny is taking *me* to the Signature Room to celebrate the New Year. Who knows, this might turn out to be *my* Holiday to Remember, if you don't mind me borrowing the title from your medley."

"Go right ahead. The Signature Room is pretty impressive. Is there any chance your Mr. Denny might finally be getting serious?"

"Not to my knowledge. Still, there's no way I'm going to pass up a date with a buff trainer from the fitness club, fireworks over Lake Michigan, and a kiss at midnight."

"A kiss at midnight," Elizabeth sighed, kind of dreamy-eyed. "Aunt Maddy says being kissed at midnight by someone special is *magical,* and although I've yet to meet that perfect someone, I believe her."

"Girl, you've been watching way too many holiday romance movies on your favorite channel, if you ask me. I could never be like you. At any rate, if you need an escort, you can always ask my brother. I know Johnny isn't ideal, but he's okay in a pinch. On second thought, what about that cute drummer from the music store? Didn't you go out with him a couple of times? Maybe you can take him."

"*George Wickham?!* I think not! And *no,* we *never* dated. Char, your memory fails you. I only agreed to sing backups for that smooth talker's band at Lollapalooza[1] last summer because he was desperate. Believe me; *dating* was *not* part of the chord chart. Besides, I'm hardly interested in a fly-by-night drummer or any freelance musician for that matter. *And* I'm definitely considering adding your brother to my *no-go* list of men. If Johnny stands me up for one more transmission or any other mechanical failure, the man is toast. As it turns out, I'll probably hand him his marching orders once he escorts me to Charles Bingley's holiday party on Friday. Who knows, I may end up following Jane's lead and using her professional dating service after all. I mean, who could complain about *Mr. Bingley?*"

"Are you serious?"

"Absolutely! Charles is exceptional. He's considerate and has a great sense of humor. Plus, he brings Jane flowers, sends her cards, and takes her out to dinner, concerts, company functions, yada, yada…. And to top it all off, it was Charles Bingley who recommended the Vocalteens for the Pemberley gig. As one of the corporate lawyers who work for the foundation, he was happy to submit my PR materials to the marketing director. Mr. Reynolds thinks our *Holiday to Remember* medley will be perfect for the charity gala."

"I agree; it's bound to be a hit. The kids are already looking pretty good, and you still have until next Thursday to pull it all together for the showcase. Speaking of the gala, I hear the CEO of Darcy Enterprises is pretty *hot.*" Charlotte wiggled her eyebrows as if in the know. "*William Darcy* has been in *all* of the tabloids lately. They say he's some kind of aloof, *mystery man*—tall, dark, and handsome. I wonder if *he'll* be there."

"*William Darcy?*" Elizabeth frowned. "His sister, Georgiana, was studying piano with Aunt Maddy at the music store until…." Her voice trailed off. "Are you sure he's connected to the foundation? Mr. Reynolds never mentioned him."

"Small world! According to Google, the foundation is run by Darcy Enterprises." Glancing at the wall clock, Charlotte changed the subject. "It looks like the bell is about to ring, so I'd better head over to my advanced ballet class. Do you still need help tonight with choreography for the opening number?"

"I'd really appreciate it, since I'm going to have my hands full with the pit orchestra. If you can take over while we run through my new arrangements, it would mean one less thing for me to juggle at practice."

"No problem. I'll be there. Catch you later."

"Thanks."

After Charlotte left, Elizabeth minimized her music program and quickly googled William Darcy, CEO of Darcy Enterprises. "I can't believe it. It *is* him! So, Mr. Darcy," she continued to babble while glaring at the computer screen. "Your Mr. Reynolds booked us for the gala. How was *he* to know you never wanted to see me again?" She shrugged her shoulders. "Oh well, I guess we'll just have to make the most of it, won't we?"

~ ♫ ~

William's office at Darcy Enterprises
A few days later

"Bingley, I've been waiting on the paperwork for the new contracts."

"All ready to go, Boss!"

"Do you have to be so cheerful when you come in here? This *is* work, you know."

"Can't help myself, Darcy. It must be love." He patted his chest with a melodramatic gesture.

"Don't tell me you've already fallen for your latest angel."

"My Janie? She *is* an angel, and yes, I'm madly in love."

William rolled his eyes. "She smiles too much, just like you, I might add. I suppose that makes the two of you *perfect* for one another."

"Ha, you should try it sometime! The holidays are practically around the corner, and you could use some diversion. You've been nothing but a bear since the end of summer."

"I've had a lot on my plate." William scowled, directing his attention to the folder Charles had just handed him.

"Speaking of plates, you *do* remember the holiday party tomorrow night at my parents' home in Winnetka, don't you? With Mom and

Dad living in Italy for the past year, the house rarely gets used. Caroline has pulled out all of the stops to impress you. She's having the party catered by some celebrity chef from the city and even hired a jazz trio to play easy listening music before dinner. Hopefully they can move on to some lively tunes afterwards, since Jane *loves* to dance." He grinned.

"Humph! Spare me the details."

"All in all, there should be about sixty or seventy from corporate along with a few other staff members in attendance. And if you're not into partying, you can always network a little and combine business with pleasure. Say, maybe you can hook up with Jane's sister, Liz. You know ... the music teacher from the performing arts school? You could hang out with her for a while and probably get some useful advice for Georgiana while you're at it."

"Her sister?" His brows furrowed. "It should be some party with both your and Jane's sister in attendance. I feel a migraine coming on just thinking about it."

"What are you talking about? Liz is nothing like Caro. You might actually like her. She's unpretentious, intelligent, and a very pretty brunette—quite unlike some of the women you've dated in the past."

"Bingley, you're wasting your time. I'm not looking for a date, and even if I were, it would *not* be with Elizabeth Bennet. For your information, we've already met, and it didn't go well. End of story."

"Suit yourself. Maybe she'll hit it off with Richard."

"Right."

"At any rate, I expect you to play nice. Per Jane's suggestion, I recommended Liz's kids to Reynolds for the foundation gala, and whether you like her or not, Ms. Bennet's top choir from her school is on the bill."

"Great," he grumbled, adding under his breath, "Serves me right for not approving the entertainment choices myself."

"O ... kay, I can tell when you're not in the mood for conversation. Just shoot me a text if you need anything else with regards to these papers."

"You can count on it."

Soon after Charles left, William deliberately pushed aside the documents and stepped to the window of his high rise office in the Chicago Loop area. Firmly grabbing one of the window sashes, he aimlessly gazed down on Lake Shore Drive and out over the chilly lake.

~ ♪ ~

August, four months earlier

In William Darcy's opinion, this particular summer was one of the worst Chicago had experienced in years. Even though it was humid, there was little rain, and the temperatures had stayed well into the nineties with no end in sight. Despite the weather, a multitude of activities continued on as usual, and people from all over the metropolitan area converged upon the city. Chicago summers offered some of the finest food and music festivals in the nation. For the moment, however, he was cooped up in the office working late while his sister attended the Lollapalooza Music Fest with some of her friends from the Latin School.[2]

"Oh, the heck with work!" William suddenly burst out in frustration. "I should have just gone along as a chaperone and tried to catch up tomorrow." As it was, he was a little uneasy knowing Grant Park was mobbed with spectators and that Mary King's mother was the only adult monitoring an enthusiastic group of teens at a rock concert. Without hesitation, William quickly shut down his laptop and began organizing his papers when his phone chimed. Frowning, he saw the call was from Mary King.

"Mr. Darcy, Georgie is gone! We can't find her anywhere. I don't know what to do," Mary sobbed.

"What do you mean you can't find her? Where are you now?"

"We're at the Rock and Rollers main stage by the cooling station west of Balboa and Michigan. We were all watching *Dragon's Lair*, one of the alternative rock bands. Georgie said she knew the drummer, George Wickham, a teacher from the music store. She disappeared after their set. We thought maybe she went to talk with him or something, but when we asked some of the guys in the band, they hadn't seen her, and her cell is going to voicemail."

"Listen, Mary, stay calm. My office is less than a mile from the Park. I'll take a cab and be there as soon as I can."

"Okay, my mom and the other kids are all looking for her. Mr. Darcy," her voice suddenly brightened. "I think I see one of the singers from the *Dragon's Lair* near the staging area. I'll see if she knows anything and get right back to you."

"Good. Call me with whatever you find out."

~ ♪ ~

"Darcy," William barked, into his phone, despite not recognizing the displayed number.

"Mr. Darcy, this is Liz Bennet. My Aunt Gardiner is your sister's piano teacher. I was performing with the *Dragon's Lair* tonight and heard from Mary King that Georgie is missing. Where are you now?"

"I'm in the park walking down Balboa towards the staging area."

"Great! I just talked with one of the sound technicians who told me he saw a girl fitting your sister's description leaving with George Wickham."

"Dear Lord," William cursed under his breath.

"Wickham's van is parked nearby in the musician's lot on one of the greens. As soon as you get here, I'll show you."

"I see Mary now." He waved and started running. "Be right there."

Moments later

"Mr. Darcy, I'm Liz Bennet. Mary, let your mom know what's going on and wait right here for her and the other kids. I'll call you or send a text as soon as we find Georgie. Mr. Darcy?" She gestured across the lawn, and the two of them took off as fast as they could maneuver through a crowd of spectators.

"Miss Bennet. How long have you known this George Wickham?" he asked tersely.

"Not long. He was recommended by one of the regular teachers from my aunt's music store and occasionally subs when he's in town. I don't mean to alarm you, but the man can be somewhat of a charmer."

"And he's teaching children at your aunt's store?!" he bellowed. "If something has happened to my sister, I swear I'll shut her down."

"Mr. Darcy, can we just remain calm and focus on finding Georgie before you threaten to put your legal team to work?" He made no response. "Wickham's van is the black one over there in the next row. It looks like the dome light is on, so hopefully she's inside." As soon as they reached the van, William jerked open the rear doors only to find his sister lying passed out on the floor with Wickham trying to shake her awake as he hovered over her.

"What did you do to her, you scum?!" William shouted, roughly shoving Wickham away from his sister and slamming him into the interior wall of the van. "I'll see you in jail for this." In the meantime, Elizabeth immediately bent over Georgiana, hoping to rouse her. Her color was ashen and her breathing faint.

"I didn't do anything. It was just a little Ketamine[3] to help her relax." He cowered in the corner, raising his arm in defense. "It's perfectly legal."

"Ketamine!" both Elizabeth and William shouted, exchanging alarmed looks.

Elizabeth pulled out her phone and immediately keyed in 911. "Yes, there is an emergency in the performer's parking lot, a little southeast of Balboa and Columbus Drive, on the green.... A teen was given Ketamine. She's unconscious and barely breathing. Her color is not good.... Elizabeth Bennet.... Yes, this is my cell.... Black van, I think Ford ... Five minutes? Please hurry. Thanks.

"Mr. Darcy, I'll text Mary King so she can let the others know we found Georgie."

"I don't want those kids anywhere near here. Do you understand me?" he snapped."

"Yes, of course," she answered coolly. "I'll wait outside for the emergency vehicles."

"You do that." He nearly spat before returning his attention to his sister.

Minutes later, the ambulance and police arrived. Wickham was detained while William accompanied Georgiana to the hospital in the ambulance. Elizabeth remained behind to deal with the police and reassure Georgiana's friends and Mrs. King that she would be okay.

~ ♪ ~

The present

"Elizabeth Bennet," William sighed, stepping away from the window. At the time, he blamed others for what had happened to his sister, but after all was said and done; he also knew Elizabeth was right. There was no one to blame but himself. He would never forget the turn of her countenance as she spoke in defense of Mrs. Gardiner following George Wickham's hearing.

"Mr. Darcy, how dare you berate my aunt?! Have you ever set foot in her studio? Have you even bothered to have a conversation with her concerning your sister's progress? Maybe she should have had better judgement in hiring George Wickham, but Madeline Gardiner is not culpable for what took place outside of the studio. And if you were not so full of yourself, perhaps you would gain a little perspective."

"Well, Ms. Bennet, it looks like we'll be seeing each other again." He massaged the back of his neck trying to relieve some of the tension he was feeling. "And ... I guess it's about time I dished out an apology for my offensive behavior."

CHAPTER 2

DINNER AT EIGHT

Bingley's holiday party
Friday night, later that week

"Lizzy, this dress is spectacular! Pretty sophisticated for a music teacher, if you ask me. It's not at all your usual style. I can't believe you rented it!" Jane stepped back giving her sister the once over.

"Shush! Do you want the whole room to know? And for your information, this is *not* the dress I rented. Take a look." She began scrolling through her phone. "*This* is the confirmation and picture of what I *should* have gotten in the mail."

"*Star in your own show in this classic dress*," Jane read aloud. "*The fold-over neckline comes to life in an off-shoulder effect. The bodice and mini-skirt are lined for a flattering fit and perfect for a hot date or night out with friends.* Lizzy, the dress they sent you is anything but a mini dress; although I will say the plunging neckline down the back of it is definitely way off the shoulder. So, what happened?"

"Elizabeth *Benton* who lives in Meryton, *Ohio* is what happened. She got *my* dress. *Rent the Modern Closet* has promised to give me a full refund. With this dress being delivered while I was at school, I wasn't able to send it back in time to get a replacement for tonight. Nevertheless, here I am in the flesh, so to speak." She struck a classy pose before playfully breaking into laughter. Elizabeth's dress was a sleek fiery red, cowl backless V-neck, floor length formal gown with a thigh-high side slit.

"You have no idea what I went through trying to find a strapless, backless, push-up, stick-on bra for this thing," she whispered. Jane tried to hide her amusement while listening to Elizabeth detailing her dilemma. "It was either go braless or be forced to wear one of my kids' show choir dresses. *Not!* Thankfully, Charlotte came to the rescue with a scandalous bra she bought from *Cleavage Designs*. She says this bra is all the rage on Instagram. Everyone is talking about it."

"*Cleavage Designs?*" Jane mouthed—her eyes wide open. "Um … I didn't think you and Charlotte were anywhere close to the same size. She's so … willowy."

"We're *not* the same size, but fortunately, there was enough wiggle room to make due." The two sisters giggled.

"Speaking of your *hot* date, where's Johnny Lucas? Is he still parking the car?" Jane scanned the room looking for Elizabeth's absentee escort.

"Oh, he's parking the car alright—in Detroit!"

"You're kidding. You mean to tell me Lucas stood you up *again?*"

"That he did!"

"What was it this time—a transmission? Someone's timing belt?"

"Jane, have you no imagination? I'm being stood up for…. And I quote—*a Classic 1966 Chevrolet Corvette—350 V8, four-speed Manual, only 96,000 Miles*—end of quote. *And* as red as my dress, I might add."

"Wow! I can imagine a Corvette must cost a pretty penny, no matter what year it was built. What kind of price tag are we talking here?"

"It was only fifty-one thousand big ones, says Mr. Lucas."

"Fifty-one thousand—as in dollars?" Jane nearly gasped. "Where does a mechanic get that kind of money?"

"Johnny and his buddy Scott got the loan approved yesterday and headed straight for Detroit after they closed up shop this afternoon."

"Oh, Lizzy, I'm so sorry. We really have to get you signed up for the…."

"Don't even say it. I promise I'll look into your dating service once the holidays are over."

"Good, I'm holding you to it. In the meantime, take heart, dear sister. With the way you look in this dress, there's bound to be some attractive single, corporate-type who will be glad to ogle you for an hour or two. Charles says he has a friend from work who is recently divorced, Richard somebody or other. He's not bringing a date, from what I gather. You never know, this may very well turn out to be *your* Holiday to Remember."

"Very funny, Jane. More like *A Holiday to Forget*! Something tells me I should seriously consider changing the name of that medley when I get back to school on Monday."

"Lizzy!"

"Enough about my love life *or* lack thereof. I meant to ask you, what's up with this strange house?"

"A bit much, isn't it?"

"The décor is so … black and white, in a sterile ultra-modern kind of way. Aside from a couple of Art Deco pictures scattered here and there, I think this place is in dire need of color. Of course, no one could ever complain about the white Steinway. It's very classy."

"The piano actually belongs to Caroline, and the house has been in the Bingley family for decades. She was the one who suggested the enclosed terrace be added on for hosting large dinner parties. I think you'll rather like it when we go in to eat later on. It looks very classy."

"I'll try to keep an open mind." She smiled.

"In general, Charles rarely comes here except to visit his parents when they're in residence, or if he wants to entertain a large group like tonight. Between you and me, he prefers his condo in the city. My only advice about the house is to stay away from the *man cave*. Bingley Senior was a big time safari hunter. The room definitely gives me the creeps, and not simply because I'm a vegetarian."

"Thanks for the warning. For now, I'd rather check out the music in the next room and mingle a little with the foundation crowd. I'm hoping to meet Mr. Reynolds, since he was the one who booked the Vocalteens for the Gala. He's been very helpful, and I'd like to thank him in person."

"I'm sure Charles would be happy to introduce the two of you. Last I saw him, he was chatting with one of his co-workers in the next room. I wonder what's keeping him."

"There's no rush."

Entering the great room, Elizabeth was ecstatic when she saw who was at the keyboard. "Jane, look! It's Skip Evans and his trio! I knew I recognized his style. Last July, he did a series of jazz workshops at Elmhurst College, and earlier in the summer, we worked together when some of my high school students attended the All State Jazz Fest at Northwestern University. Skip is such an amazing musician. One of my seniors has been studying privately with him. How about I introduce you to the guys?"

"Thanks, but I think I'll go find Charles. You go ahead and have some fun and we'll catch up in a bit."

~ ♪ ~

A little later

"William, can you tell me *who* is the gorgeous brunette talking with the piano player?" Richard Fitzwilliam let out a low growl, unable to contain his desires.

"What?" William's gaze barely acknowledged his cousin's inquiry, totally mesmerized by the woman he at one time practically vowed to ruin, along with her aunt.

"Man, she's hot. Do you see her bare back? And that slit...." He let out a low whistle. "Did I ever mention how much I really enjoy long legs? Uh ... earth to Darcy?" Richard nudged William's arm.

"The *woman* you happen to be lusting after is none other than Miss Elizabeth Bennet."

"You've got to be kidding. Not the backup singer from Lollapalooza who was with that Wickham character? Isn't she the one who nearly chewed your head off after Georgie testified at the hearing?"

"One and the same, only it turns out … she wasn't *with* George Wickham after all. Miss Bennet was only helping out that sleaze since he had been subbing as a teacher at her aunt's music store. My investigators thoroughly checked out both women, and I found I was utterly wrong in my assumptions. In fact, I still owe each of them an apology."

"A little belated if you ask me."

"I know."

"Well, considering this *pertinent* bit of information, I think I'll get going. I wouldn't want to jeopardize my own chances with such a beautiful woman by being associated with *you*. Hopefully, she won't remember me from the hearing. Besides, it looks like dear *Caro* is about to make her move in this direction, and I'd only be in her way." He chuckled. "You better hope she didn't notice your gawking or you'll never hear the end of it." William rolled his eyes in disgust. "Wish me luck, buddy!"

~ ♪ ~

"William, darling, what are you doing over here in this corner all by yourself? Waiting for me by any chance?" Caroline purred while running her hand along his biceps.

"Nothing really," he answered coolly. "Just nursing my drink, as you can see." He purposely stepped aside, forcing Caroline to stop groping his arm.

Caroline immediately frowned when she realized who had been taking up William's attention. "Oh, for pity's sake!" she fumed. "That woman is nothing more than a high school music teacher, *hardly* worth your notice. There's no money to speak of in the Bennet family, and her father is nothing but a literature professor at some junior college or other.

"Frankly, I don't know what's gotten into Charles lately. His *sweet*

Janie, a little nobody nurse from Meryton Heights has his head spinning. She's only after his money, and *now* here is her tag-along sister who is just as eager to trap some unsuspecting guy." Putting down her drink, Caroline stepped directly in front of William with the intent of blocking his view of Elizabeth. Taking hold of his free hand and pulling it to her bosom she moved closer. "William, I can guarantee you'll have much more fun hanging out with me, tonight. I have some new *art-work* worth viewing in my bedroom, if you take my meaning." She batted her eye lashes while managing to stroke his calf with the side of her stiletto shoe.

"I think not, Caroline." He scowled, detaching himself from her once again. "And … for your information, I find *nothing* wrong with the Bennet sisters. Now, if you will excuse me, I need to speak with Reynolds." William turned and walked away without saying anything further.

"I always did like a challenge," she mumbled under her breath. "And I'm certainly not going to let someone like *Eliza Bennet* step on my toes tonight."

~ ♫ ~

Meanwhile Elizabeth was commiserating with Skip Evans who was rolling out the last riff on the keyboard before finishing the set. "Nice arrangement," she offered. "A touch of Oscar Peterson?"

"There's no fooling you, Liz. Peterson's arrangements are classic. Say, how would you like to sit in with the guys for a little while? We only have one more set before dinner is served, but I really need to call Carrie. She hasn't been feeling well and sent me a text not too long ago."

"How's she doing?"

"The OB says it could be any day now, and she's been having false labor pains all week—kind of unnerving."

"Move over. I'm happy to help out. Give Carrie my best. Who knows, if Eric and Alex cooperate, I'll even sing lead." She gave them a wink.

"You go for it, sweetie, and we'll finish off with a duet when I come back."

"Great! So what will it be, guys? I see Skip left us with *You are the Sunshine of my Life.* Are we good to go?" They both agreed, so Elizabeth plunged right in with the intro and began singing the first verse. Her energy seemed to fill the room, and before long Richard, along with several others, had gathered around the musicians to make requests. Once Skip returned, he made good on his promise for a duet and asked if anyone had a particular song they would like to hear. Stepping forward, Richard leaned in and suggested, "How about *When I fall in Love?*"

"Ah, I see we have a true romantic in our midst." Elizabeth flashed him an inviting smile before turning to Skip who nodded in agreement. Skip began by playing the intro to an arrangement of the song which was worked up for singer Natalie Cole. She happened to perform it with virtual clips sung by her father, the famous Nat King Cole, some years back. Taking the mic in hand, Elizabeth positioned herself front and center.

Starting out with the beguiling melody of this old Jazz standard, the mood was immediately set as Elizabeth began singing the familiar words of the tune in her low rich alto voice. With her eyes half-closed, she swayed to the music while she and Skip alternately sang the melody and filled in with velvety harmonies.

And the moment
I can feel that you feel that way too
Is when I fall in love
With you.

When I Fall in Love – by Victor Young and Edward Heyman

Little by little, those who had been milling about and chatting nearby stopped what they were doing to listen. It was as though each observer fell completely under her spell, not knowing if it was the shimmering red dress, her smoky voice, or a combination of both which pulled them in. Unknown to Elizabeth, William Darcy was equally captivated. His gaze narrowed until it seemed she was the center of his world. In a way, Charles was right. She actually was quite different from the usual women he dated—business type, often superficial, and only interested in his money.

Elizabeth Bennet was extraordinary. With her open demeanor and unassuming nature, she had a zest for life which seemed to spill forth at every turn. She was a talented musician who was devoted to her students and a woman who was fiercely loyal to her family, as was proven by her defense of Mrs. Gardiner when they exchanged heated words back in early October. If they could resolve their differences, William wondered whether or not Elizabeth would be able see past the corporate façade he generally portrayed in the business world and look at him for the man he truly was.

When her eyes finally drifted to where William was standing, she gave him a half-smile, and his heart felt as though it might have skipped a beat. Her eyes were warm and filled with passion as she continued to sing. Could she possibly know what he was thinking? No, she was only caught up in the sentiment of the song, nothing more. Moments later, she turned away and finished singing as elegantly as she had begun. As the two singers concluded, not a sound could be heard in the room until the last chord on the keyboard finished resonating.

The crowd burst into applause and though the set was finished, everybody asked for one more number. Elizabeth was embarrassed by the adulation and turned to Skip for a suggestion. "Okay, if you insist," she responded. "One last song, and then the trio will take a break until after dinner. This past June, Skip Evans and I worked with a very talented group of high school students at the All State Jazz Fest. They performed a well-loved—though admittedly *cheesy* song—at the final concert. We give you, *I will survive*—the hit song made famous by Gloria Gaynor and first performed in 1978. Get out your disco shoes and let's party!"

Skip started out with the all too familiar piano intro, and Elizabeth immediately took on a classic pose with *attitude*. She sang with spunk, inspiring the crowd to join in not only with dancing, but with singing as the song progressed. At the end, the room was filled with exuberant applause and many happy faces.

Oh, no, not I, I will survive
Oh as long as I know how to love, I know I'm still alive
I've got my life to live, and I've got all my love to give
And I'll survive, I will survive

I will survive – by Freddie Perren and Dino Fekaris

Caroline nearly exploded when she happened to walk back into the great room during the height of Elizabeth's performance. Seething, she sidled up to William and complained through gritted teeth, "Can you believe her nerve? This is *my* party and that little nobody is trying to take over like she owns the place."

"Actually, Caroline, this is *Charles'* party, and it looks to me like everyone is having fun. Let's face it … Elizabeth Bennet is one talented performer, and she knows how to work the crowd."

"Well, for your information, *I* was the one who hired Skip Evans and his trio. Their job was to play easy listening music before dinner and not carry on with some high school show choir exhibition. Frankly, I see nothing special about that woman!" she fumed.

"It's her eyes," William murmured. "Every word she sings seems to come alive in her eyes when she's performing."

"Her what?!" Caroline interrupted. "You listen to me, William Darcy! If I wanted to stand up there and make a singing fool of myself, I could easily do it. For your information, I happen to have far more integrity than to allow myself to be degraded in such a manner."

"Really? I didn't know you sang."

"Well of course I don't sing. But when I studied music at the conservatory, my professors all said I was multi-talented. I could have pursued an operatic career if I so chose, but *classical piano* happened to be my major. Once this song is finished, I'm sending everyone out to the terrace for dinner. *And* let me tell you, I had better not see that want-to-be *Jazz Queen* singing when I open up the floor for dancing. I won't stand for it! By the way, we're at table one. Wait for me, and we'll go in together."

"Caroline…." She stalked off in a huff, ready to grab hold of the mic and make her announcement as soon Skip played the final chord. William, on the other hand, ran his fingers through his hair in exasperation and wondered what he ever did to deserve being stalked by one of the most irritating women of his acquaintance. *This could prove to be a very long night.* Adding to his frustration, he could see Richard was about to make his move on Elizabeth. Assuming the two of them would be dining together and with Caroline literally breathing down his neck, his apology would have to wait until later.

CHAPTER 3

AND THE BEAT GOES ON

Bingley's party continues

Once the well-wishers had begun to make their way out onto the terrace for dinner, Richard stepped forward. "Ms. Bennet, you were awesome, and I can't begin to tell you how much I'm looking forward to hearing your choir perform at the Foundation Gala."

"Thank you. My students are exceptionally talented. Please, call me Liz. And you are…."

"I'm Richard Fitzwilliam—Director of Human Resources at Darcy Enterprises." He held out his hand, which she reluctantly shook on hearing the Darcy name.

Her face sobered as she arched an eyebrow in his direction. "I thought you looked familiar. I seem to recall seeing you at George Wickham's hearing, and if I am not mistaken, you are a relation of *Mr. William Darcy?*"

"Yes." He uncomfortably cleared his throat. "It seems my cousin's abrasive manner from that particular day has not been forgotten. He's really not so bad once you break through his gruff exterior. Mind you, I'm not making any excuses. Darcy just happens to be a little intense when it comes to his sister."

"Is that so? I assume your definition of *intense* includes being judgmental and arrogant to the point of being rude?"

"I plead the fifth." He threw up his hands. "The truth is my cousin doesn't always make a great first impression. Can we leave it at that and start again?"

She studied him for a few moments before answering, "If you like."

"Thank you. I was actually hoping you might join me for dinner."

"Alright, if you promise to answer a few questions I have about the Foundation and at some point introduce me to Mr. Reynolds. I've yet to meet him."

"Then you're in luck! It so happens we'll be sitting at the Reynolds' table, and I would be more than happy to introduce the two of you. You'll like Bob. He's the backbone of our charities."

"Good. I've wanted to personally thank Mr. Reynolds ever since he booked my students to perform at the Gala."

"It will be my pleasure to make the introduction." He grinned and willingly escorted Elizabeth out onto the terrace.

~ ♪ ~

Dinner on the heated terrace proved to be an elegant affair. Elizabeth was delighted to finally meet Bob Reynolds, and secretly reveled in the sumptuous five-course catered experience. The French cuisine had an Italian flair, and Elizabeth could not remember eating a tastier meal. Influenced by lively conversation, she was even inclined to admire the extravagant black and white decor, to which Caroline had added lavish gold accents and potted plants, reminiscent of the Ritz-Carlton in Chicago.

Two tables away, however, a resentful William Darcy was forced to endure demands and complaints of Caroline Bingley throughout the entire meal. He often wondered how someone as likeable a Charles could be related to such a woman. If it wasn't for a strong family resemblance, he would have sworn Caroline was switched at birth. She would not stop fawning over him with provocative conversation and her braggadocious demeanor had soured his appetite long before the food was even served. At this point, William couldn't care less about the bouillabaisse soup or vegetable ratatouille or saignant steak cooked in flavorful wine and herbs.

Other than attempting to carry on a reasonable conversation with Charles and Jane, his only pleasure came from an occasional glance at the beautiful woman who was unreservedly conversing with his cousin. While he couldn't catch any of their conversation, he noted the way her eyes sparkled and how her infectious laughter seemed to light up the entire table. *What a pity I offended her all those months ago. Elizabeth Bennet would have made a delightful dinner companion.*

~ ♪ ~

Following the meal, the guests leisurely returned to the main house, where conversations continued and the dancing was about to begin. As soon as Caroline excused herself to speak with the caterers, William took the opportunity to seek out Elizabeth. Richard had temporarily vacated his seat and was talking with one of his associates at another table. William wondered if she would even listen to what he had to say, since their last conversation still left a bitter taste in his mouth.

Approaching the table, William politely greeted Bob Reynolds and his co-workers before singling out Elizabeth. "Miss Bennet," he quietly interjected taking Richard's seat. "May I please have a few minutes of your time?" His mien was serious.

"Mr. Darcy." She stiffened and coolly replied, "Uh … yes, of course."

"If you don't mind, could we speak in the library? I would prefer our conversation to be private."

"As you wish."

William helped Elizabeth with her chair and motioned to the hallway saying, "It's this way." Moments later, they were in the library, which unlike the rest of the house was quiet, save for the crackling of logs in the wood-burning fireplace.

"May I get you a drink?" he offered. "There's a small refrigerator with cool beverages and a wine cabinet if you would care for something."

"No, thank you, Mr. Darcy. I had more than enough at dinner, and other than water with lemon, I rarely drink unless it's a special occasion."

"Miss Bennet...."

"Liz, please," she interrupted. "This formality is not necessary."

"Very well, then I prefer you call me William." She nodded, and they both took a seat on the sofa.

"For some time, I've wanted to apologize for my unreasonable behavior towards you and your aunt." William unconsciously tapped his fingertips on his thigh. "I overreacted, and there was no excuse on my part for the unfeeling way either of you were treated by me or my staff during the incident with George Wickham. I hope my accusations didn't cause any undue distress for Mrs. Gardiner."

"Thank you. I admit it *was* a trying time for her, and the studio did suffer a little because of the unwanted publicity."

"I'm so sorry to hear it."

"Nevertheless, everything is back to normal now. I appreciate your candor and will be happy to convey your apology."

"You were right, you know. If I had been more diligent when it came to my sister's safety, the entire incident might have been avoided." He sighed. "Since our parents' sudden death, it has been difficult. Although we have other family members who live in the area, my sister tends to view me more as a father figure than an older brother. For nearly four years, I've been solely responsible for Georgie, but in this instance...." He shook his head. "My parents would have been horrified."

"Mr. Darcy ... William..." Elizabeth briefly touched his hand. "I'm so sorry for your loss. At dinner, Bob Reynolds explained what happened to your parents and how the proceeds from the Foundation Gala are given to *Mothers Against Drunk Driving* in support of families who have suffered similar losses. Until tonight, I had no idea your own family were victims. With Georgie being so young, I can understand why you reacted as you did."

"Even though my sister is a junior in high school, she is only fifteen. Because she skipped a grade, most of her friends from the Latin School are one or two years older. Last summer, I lashed out at everyone who was involved. I'd been working long hours, and Georgie, being out of school, obviously needed more of my time and was often bored. At the last minute, I foolishly allowed her to attend the festival without thoroughly checking out the plans. While Mrs. King arranged the transportation, I didn't know there would be no other adult supervision until the day of the event. I could have easily put aside my work for one evening and assisted Mary's mother. In the end, it was my own negligence that caused my sister harm."

"Possibly, but as a teacher of high school students, I know from first-hand experience you cannot be with your children twenty-four-seven. It doesn't matter how bright your child is or how caring you are as a parent, every single day there is an opportunity for something to happen. We can only try to do our best and pray our young people will remember our advice and rely on common sense to see them through difficult situations."

"Thank you. I appreciate your kind words."

"How is Georgie doing now?"

"I'm sorry to say, not particularly well. After what happened last summer, she refused to go back to the Latin School. She said she couldn't face the humiliation."

"Oh, no. She must be very lonely without her friends."

"She is. Bob Reynolds' wife, Betty, whom you met at dinner, has been supervising Georgie's home-school lessons. She's a former school teacher and has been invaluable. But other than interacting with Mrs. Reynolds, my sister pretty much keeps to herself. She still refuses to see any of her old classmates, and on top of everything, I haven't found a new piano teacher to replace your aunt. So far, I've had three different teachers come to our home, but none of them have worked out. As you can imagine, Georgie was quite attached to Mrs. Gardiner. I'm kind of at a loss as to what I should do."

"May I make a suggestion?"

"By all means."

"Well, you know I teach at the Meryton Academy for the Performing Arts in the city, right?"

"Yes."

"Admission to our school is based on merit and talent. I've heard your sister play, and she is very gifted. If Georgie is willing, I could arrange an audition for her before the next semester begins. Assuming she is accepted, your sister could start in mid-January with the new term. Aunt Gardiner teaches privately at the school two days a week. Georgie could easily resume lessons with her or possibly try one of the other piano teachers if she prefers."

William shook his head. "It never even occurred to me to look for an alternative school such as the music academy."

"Why don't we exchange numbers now and talk more about what the school has to offer over the weekend?"

"I'd like that, if it wouldn't be an imposition."

"Not in the least." Taking out their phones, Elizabeth continued, "If Georgie likes my suggestion, the two of you can check out our webpage, and I'll be happy to answer any questions you might have. If you're able to bring her to the academy one afternoon next week, it will be the perfect time to watch some of our performing groups rehearsing for the December Showcase."

"This sounds too good to be true. Liz, you are a life saver. How can I ever thank you?"

"Don't. Let's just see how it all works out first. Do we have a deal?" Elizabeth extended her hand.

"We do!" They shook on it. "I can't begin to tell you how good I feel about your recommendations—relieved, actually. Listen, how about we put this aside for now and head on back to the party? I hear some great Latin music being played, and I'm not at all averse to dancing tonight." He smiled broadly, bringing his dimples into full view as he pulled her to her feet.

"The stoic Mr. Darcy dances?" she teased.

"It's been a few years, but I'll have you know my parents loved ballroom dancing and *insisted* I take lessons when I was growing up. I imagine I can still shuffle through a fox-trot or even a cha-cha if you're up to it. On second thought…." His eyes slowly traversed the length of her body in her tempting red dress. "Do you by any chance … *tango?*"

"Tango?!" She flashed him a smile full of mischief. "Mr. Darcy, it so happens I do!"

"Well then, Miss Bennet … the night is young and the music awaits us. Shall we?" William held out his hand and eagerly led Elizabeth from the library to the great room where the trio was currently playing *Quiet Nights and Quiet Stars,* an old classic by Antonio Carlos Jobim from 1960. Pulling her into his embrace, the couple moved in tandem as they flawlessly executed the sensual steps of a *Bossa nova.* Although it was not a tango, the Latin rhythms pulled both Elizabeth and William into the alluring wonder of the music.

CHAPTER 4

CARO'S REVENGE

The room itself wasn't particularly warm, but each time William took Elizabeth through a turn and pulled her into his embrace, the heat emanating between the two dancers only increased. For William, the feel of her bare back was nearly his undoing. Her skin was warm and soft, and every time he touched her, fiery surges ignited his entire body. With their eyes never leaving one another, his urge to taste her tempting red lips only grew stronger.

"William, I think you downplayed the extent of those youthful dance lessons," Elizabeth said, attempting to break some of the physical tension which was building between them.

"Perhaps I'm simply inspired by the beautiful woman I'm holding in my arms," he returned causing her to blush. "In general, I rarely dance, but having you for my partner…. Well, let's say I definitely would like to see if we can manage the *tango* before the night is over."

"Then we should go ahead and put in our request. Skip can play almost anything, you know."

"I'm not saying I'm an expert even though I attended many a class at my parents' insistence. They were obsessed with the *Argentine tango*. One year they even dragged Georgie and me along with Richard and his parents to Buenos Aires, where they studied with a master teacher and actually participated in a dance exhibition."

"Buenos Aires?! I'm impressed! I take it then, Richard dances, too? He didn't mention a thing at dinner."

"Back then, Richard hated dancing and refused the lessons. When we were in Argentina, he spent most of his time trying to charm the local beauties. My cousin, more or less, has two left feet—although he'll try to make a good showing out on the floor."

"I'll remember that." Her eyes twinkled in amusement. "All in all, it must have been a very exciting trip for your family."

"Well, at the time, being a teenager and looking after my little sister while my cousin was off having fun didn't leave me particularly enthused. But now, with my parents no longer alive, I find it's one of my fondest memories. I'll never forget the way they looked at one another when they danced." He shook his head as if to put off the melancholy of the memory.

"William...." She reached up and touched his cheek.

"It's alright, Liz," he said, seeing the compassion in her eyes. He turned his head and lightly kissed her fingers before boldly taking her through another combination. By the end of the dance, William could hardly bear to part from Elizabeth. Refusing to let go of her hand he asked, "What do you think? Should we sit the next one out, or dare we go over and make our request?"

Before Elizabeth could reply, the trio began playing *Sway*—a more up-tempo song with another Latin beat. They smiled at each other and both said *Cha Cha* at the same time. Seconds later William and Elizabeth were again dancing, and nothing else seemed to matter except their connection as they moved effortlessly about the dance floor.

When we dance you have a way with me
Stay with me, sway with me
Other dancers may be on the floor Dear,
But my eyes will see only you...

Sway by Luis Demetrio—1953

"William, I can't remember when I've had this much fun dancing!" Elizabeth exclaimed when the song finished.

"The pleasure was all mine, believe me." His smile was disarming. "Come on, I see Charles and Jane. How about we go chat with them for a few minutes?"

"What? Am I wearing you out, Mr. Darcy?" she teased.

"I think not, Miss Bennet. As I said earlier, *the night is young.*" He squeezed her hand.

"Darcy," called Charles. "I see you finally took my advice and decided to enjoy yourself for a change. For one who doesn't dance much, you were pretty convincing out there." William shot him a pointed look, a little embarrassed by the compliment.

"Charles is right!" Jane added with enthusiasm. "Watching you two is like watching *Dancing with the Stars.*"

"Stop," Elizabeth nearly pleaded. "We were just having fun, right William?"

"Absolutely!"

"In fact, we were about to ask Skip if the trio would play a *tango*." The two grinned at each other in anticipation of the dance.

"Say, wasn't the tango a favorite of your parents?" Charles questioned.

"It was."

Charles leaned in to William saying, "Of course you do realize Caroline will be stalking you once she hears a *tango* being played. In fact I'm surprised she isn't out on the floor right now." William frowned. "Don't worry, we'll keep Caro busy while you two have a go, won't we, Janie?"

"Uh, yes, I suppose." She sounded a little uncertain.

"Liz, I think now would be a good time to put in our request with the trio. Can I get you anything to drink while I'm at it?"

"Some cold seltzer water with lemon would be great."

"I'll be right back."

~ ♪ ~

William was happy to leave behind any conversation concerning Caroline Bingley, and after talking with Skip for a few minutes, he went on to the bar for drinks. As he was leaving a tip for the bartender, Richard appeared at his side.

"Tell me, how is it you managed to corner the market with *the Lady in Red* out on the dance floor? For a guy who seldom dances, you sure cut some pretty mean moves."

"Richard, it's not my fault you never stuck with the lessons. Elizabeth Bennet is an amazing partner." He couldn't help but smile as he looked over in her direction.

"I suppose I can always fall back on the box-step, or if they play one of those electric slides, I should be able to follow along. Hopefully, she'll cut me a little slack."

"Please...." William rolled his eyes.

"Uh ... I hate to say it, but it looks like Caroline is on the loose, or to put it more accurately, *is* loose. Gad, I wonder how many of those margaritas she's had tonight. The woman can barely walk a straight line."

"Let's go. I don't trust her around Liz."

As soon as Caroline reached Elizabeth, Jane and Bingley, she started mouthing off. "Eliza Bennet," she slurred. "How dare you monopolize William Darcy on the dance floor? He's with *me* tonight, and I *insist* you back off." She pointed an unsteady finger at Elizabeth, who was stunned by Caroline's outburst.

"Caroline," Charles interrupted, taking her arm. "I think you've had a little too much to drink. How about we go to the kitchen and get you some strong coffee?"

"Let go of me, Charles," she hissed. Jerking her arm out of his grasp, she started to lose her balance and accidently sloshed her frozen margarita down the front of Elizabeth's dress, causing her to cry out in alarm.

"Caroline, look what you've done!" Charles nearly yelled. "Jane, please take Liz to the bathroom, and Caro, *you* are coming with me!"

"I'm not going anywhere—I've done nothing wrong!"

Just then, William and Richard reached the group, adding to the confusion. Seeing William, Caroline railed against him by spouting a series of obscenities and slanderous language before Charles could again take his sister in hand and forcibly escort her to the kitchen with Richard's help.

~ ♪ ~

The Bathroom

"Lizzy, I can't believe what happened out there. One minute we were all having such a nice time and the next…."

"Jane, *Caroline* is what happened. Ugh! You have no idea how disgusting this sticky bra feels!" exclaimed Elizabeth as she dropped the shoulder straps of her dress and tried to wiggle free of the cold, wet clingy fabric. "I hate to say it, but I'm afraid this dress is ruined, not to mention Charlotte's bra."

"Here, let me help." The two women gingerly pulled the sticky cups from Elizabeth's breasts and dropped the bra into the sink where Jane started washing off the goo in warm water. "Lizzy, you go ahead and take a shower. I'll see what I can do about the dress once I finish up with the bra."

"Thanks, Sis. What would I do without you?" Elizabeth wrapped her long hair into a bath towel, pulled off her shoes and panties, and stepped into a nice hot shower.

A few minutes later Jane called out, "Lizzy, the bra is pretty hopeless and the dress isn't looking much better. Should I see if Caroline has something you can borrow?"

"Over my dead body, Jane Bennet! I'll go naked under my coat if I have to."

"Let's hope it doesn't come to that." Jane continued to work on the dress. "Maybe I can scrounge up something from one of the servers. Too bad this had to happen. It's not quite midnight, and the party seems like it might go on for a while."

Elizabeth stepped out of the shower and wrapped herself in a fluffy towel. "At dinner, Richard told me Caroline is obsessed with William, but I never expected this. Accident or not, the woman has been giving me the *evil eye* all evening. I don't understand it. Up until a few hours ago, William and I weren't even speaking."

"That may be, but the two of you sure made up for it on the dance floor."

Elizabeth blushed. "He really is a great dancer. Aside from Caroline ruining my dress, I never expected to have such a good time tonight."

"Cheer up. Maybe he'll ask you out."

"Maybe." She shrugged.

"What do you think?" Jane held up the dress.

"No way! Please see what you can find. At this point, I'm desperate."

Jane hugged her sister. "I'll be right back. Keep the door locked."

"Don't worry about that. You're the only person here with an admission ticket."

Ten minutes later Jane returned with a waiter's jacket and Elizabeth's coat and bag. "Lizzy, it's me. You can unlock the door now."

"Thank goodness. What did you find?" Jane held up the jacket. "It looks a little big, but I'll manage. My crazy faux fur is so long it'll hide just about anything."

"William was waiting in the hall. He feels really bad about what happened. I gave him your keys so he could bring your car around. It started snowing."

"William?" She blushed. "I'm so embarrassed."

"Don't be. He likes you."

"You really think so?"

"I do."

"I hope so." She shyly smiled. "Now let me see what I can do with this jacket." Elizabeth put on the server's coat while Jane rolled up the dress and stuffed it into her bag, along with the soggy bra.

"Good luck with this mess when you get home."

"Thanks, I'll need it," said Elizabeth wrapping her coat tightly about her body and firmly tying the belt in place so her lack of clothing wouldn't show. "I guess this is the best I can do, so *let's get the heck out of Dodge* before something else happens to me tonight!" The two sisters hugged and Jane opened the door. No one seemed to pay much attention as they made their way to the foyer where William was anxiously waiting. As soon as he saw the two women, he immediately stepped forward and took Elizabeth's hand.

"Don't worry, Jane, I'll make sure Liz gets off okay."

"Thanks, William. Call me tomorrow, Lizzy. Love you!"

"Love you too."

~ ♪ ~

Outside

"William, thank you so much for getting my car. I had no idea it was snowing, and here I thought it was supposed to be a clear night."

"Hopefully, it's only a little lake effect snow and won't last long. Let me help you down the stairs—they're pretty slippery."

"Wow! You can say that again. I can barely keep my balance in these heels." William snuggly wrapped his arm around Elizabeth in her fluffy coat as she gripped his free hand.

"Charles will have to get these stairs salted before anyone else leaves the party."

"Well, at least I've got plenty of padding if we fall." She tightly clung to his arm as they continued to slowly take the stairs one at a time.

William chuckled. "This is some coat. I feel like I'm hugging a stuffed animal with you tucked under my arm."

"It's faux fur, you know. Jane being on the verge of a hard-core vegan insisted I get it a couple of years back, and with our Chicago winters, I'm so glad I did."

"I completely understand." He opened the door for Elizabeth, helping her into the car. Leaning over the doorframe he continued, "My mom was a vegetarian and supported several grass roots animal rights groups. To this day, Georgie insists on having a healthy supply of faux fur in her closet." A gust of wind blew the snow right past William's body causing Elizabeth to shiver.

"I'm sorry—I'll shut the door," he apologized. "Would you care if I joined you for a few minutes?"

"Please do! Come on in and warm up."

William closed her door and went to the passenger's side. Opening the door, he dusted off some of the snow and just missed bumping his head on the frame as he ducked and adjusted the seat for his long legs. "Whew, I made it."

"Sorry, I guess the Cavalier wasn't exactly made for a *tall* fellow like you," she teased, turning on the dome light.

"Yes, the hazards of the Darcy genes have been known to play havoc on my body in confined places." He chuckled.

"I've actually had this car since college, but I haven't had the heart to part with it yet. It's kind of like having an old friend."

"I know what you mean. It's easy to get attached to things when they hold fond memories."

"Still, I wouldn't mind having a newer car, especially with Bluetooth technology. Jane has it in her car, and it's so convenient when driving around the city."

"Liz…." William reached for her hand. "I'm so sorry about the way Caroline acted and what she did to your dress. I hope it's not ruined."

"It probably is, but don't worry. It was rented *and* fully insured.

"Rented?"

"Rented! And truthfully, I don't even feel guilty since they sent me the wrong dress to begin with."

"The wrong dress?" He still looked puzzled.

"My friend Charlotte Lucas says it's all the rage now. You rent a dress you could never afford to buy and select something new whenever a special occasion comes along. Charlotte is very practical in that way. If you and Georgie are able to visit the academy next week, I'll introduce her to you."

"I look forward to meeting her."

"Char teaches ballet there, and my younger sister, Kitty, says she's an outstanding instructor. Kitty and two other students from our school are members of the student company with the Joffrey Ballet and were chosen to perform in several of the Nutcracker Matinees at the Auditorium Theatre this season."

"What a coincidence. I took Georgie to see a Sunday matinee right after Thanksgiving."

"Then you would have seen my sister, although members of the *flowers corps* tend to look pretty much the same. Kitty is also a junior, and I could easily arrange for her to be excused from class and serve as a student ambassador when you tour the academy. I'm sure Georgie would enjoy meeting someone in her grade."

"I agree. I can't imagine my sister not being receptive to the idea of the school. May I call you tomorrow after we talk?"

"Absolutely! And if Georgie has any questions for me, feel free to put her on the phone. I'd be happy to speak with her. William, don't worry. I know this will work out." She squeezed his hand.

"I hope so." He paused. "There is one other thing. I overheard what Caroline said before your dress was ruined, and I wanted you to know I was *not* her date tonight. We are *not* together nor have we *ever* been."

"I never got that impression. In fact, I can easily sympathize with your plight as I have one *Billy Collins*, an IT guy from my school who thinks he has a similar claim on me. Unlike Caroline, however, he would *never* dream of spilling a drink down the front of my dress." She chuckled. "It seems he would rather talk me to death with computer jargon."

"Billy Collins?" he guardedly asked.

"Yes, and you'll get a chance to meet him first hand at the Foundation Gala. He'll be acting as my sound man for the choir that night."

"So ... you're not bringing a date to the party?" He unconsciously frowned, waiting for her answer.

"No. I figured I'd be too busy with the Vocalteens performing, plus earlier tonight, Skip Evans asked if I would do a set with the band. All things considered, I probably wouldn't make a very good date."

"Well...." He sheepishly smiled. "I tend to disagree. Actually, Miss Bennet, I was thinking you might make the perfect date for me. After all, we never did get to dance our *tango*. Would you care if I was your escort?"

"Does this mean you're asking me out, Mr. Darcy?"

"It does."

"Thank you, I accept." She beamed causing him to smile in return.

"I think you'll really enjoy the gala, and don't worry about being with your choir or singing with the band—we'll work it out as we go along."

"I can hardly wait."

"I'm glad." William momentarily checked the time on her dashboard and reluctantly said, "Well, I suppose I better let you get home. It's already midnight."

"Midnight?" She unconsciously swallowed and looked helplessly into his baby blues unable to say any more. When he reached over and caressed her cheek with his fingertips, Elizabeth couldn't help but tilt her face into his touch. Seconds later, he leaned in, placing a long soft kiss on her lips.

"That was nice," he whispered before pulling back. "Drive carefully—the roads could be slippery." She nodded, still caught up in the magic of their kiss.

"Promise you'll either text or call me as soon as you get home, okay?

"I promise."

"Goodnight, Liz. Drive carefully."

"I will. Goodnight, William."

~ ♪ ~

The drive home from Bingley's party was slow-going with the blustery lake-effect snow increasing and taking over every inch of the roadways. This was the first heavy snow of the season, and as far as Elizabeth could tell, the city had yet to get out the snowplows and salt trucks. She sighed in relief when she didn't get stuck on the side streets after finally reaching Meryton Heights. Although she kept a pair of tennis shoes on the back seat of her car, the thought of trudging through the snow or having to dig out of a drift was not appealing, especially considering she was wearing little more than her faux fur.

Elizabeth assumed William was frantic with worry because he had sent her three texts which she didn't dare answer while driving on such treacherous roads. Nor did she want to pull over in order to respond for fear of getting stuck. All of Illinois had strict laws about not texting or talking on cell phones while driving, and it wasn't until two hours later, parked in the lot across from her apartment, that she was finally able to return his call.

"Liz, where are you?" William immediately answered when he saw her number light up his phone.

"I just now got home, and I'm still sitting in my car. The driving was horrid. And with the falling temperatures and the way the wind is blowing, everything is turning into a sheet of ice." She could hear William groan in the background.

"Thank God you're alright. I was so worried when you didn't answer any of my texts. I could kick myself for not taking you home in my car. A four-wheel-drive would have been much safer on the roads than your little Cavalier."

"I can't argue with that. Thankfully, the traffic was light, but as usual, Chicago Streets and Sanitation are way behind schedule. With the ice and drifting snow, I barely made it into the parking lot. I'm just now putting on my sneakers so I can get out of the car and navigate my way across the street."

"If this keeps up, would you like me to come by tomorrow and help dig you out?"

"Don't worry. We have an arrangement with an industrious teenager in my building who is always looking for some extra spending money. He'll be out bright and early clearing the walk, and I'll ask him to take care of my car. How was your drive home?"

"With the threat of heavy snow, the party broke up shortly after you left. I was planning to spend the night in Winnetka, but with Caroline's earlier behavior, I decided to take my chances and head back to the city. Once I got to Lake Shore Drive, it wasn't so bad.

Unlike your route home, the Outer Drive had been plowed and salted."

"That was lucky."

"Well ... I guess I better let you go so you can get into your apartment and warm up. Liz?"

"Yes?"

"I'm glad we were able to patch things up between us. I still feel bad about what happened over the summer, and I hope I'll be able to apologize to your aunt in person."

"In that case, Mr. Darcy, I might happen to have one little idea simmering on the back burner which would accommodate your wish."

"Oh?"

"Let me see what I can do in the morning, and we'll talk further after you speak with Georgie."

"I'd appreciate it. Liz, be careful crossing the street. Just take your time. I wouldn't want you to slip and fall on the ice."

"Not a chance. I'll be taking baby steps, and if I happen to slip, at least I have my faux fur to break the fall."

"Good. I'll call you in the morning. Sweet dreams."

"Sweet dreams to you, too, William."

CHAPTER 5

THE MAGIC OF MUSIC

Elizabeth's Apartment
Saturday, 9 December
Late morning

Elizabeth sat at her computer drinking a cup of hot chocolate while making a few minor adjustments to the instrumental parts for the Vocalteen medley. Rehearsals for the December Showcase had been going well, and everyone was looking forward to Thursday night's performance. Hoping William and Georgiana would be able to attend, she eagerly awaited his call. A broad smile graced her lips when she remembered how caring he had been after her fiasco with Caroline. And then there was his tender kiss. "William," she sighed. What was it about him that pulled at her heartstrings?

Moments later, Elizabeth's phone chimed. Seeing it was William and that he was using a live phone chat feature, she quickly released the clip from her hair and sat up straight, hoping to look presentable. Thank goodness she wasn't working in her pajamas, which was often the case on Saturday.

"Good morning, William! How's everything? Have you been able to speak with Georgie yet?"

"Yes, we had a nice long talk, and she's very excited about visiting the academy next week."

"Great! I'll send the dean an email to give him a head's up and if you like, I can try to schedule a meeting for you and Georgie when I go in on Monday. Does Tuesday work for you?"

"Tuesday should be fine. I don't have any pressing meetings until later in the week so I can easily clear my calendar."

"Excellent!"

"You know, Liz, after talking with Georgie, I realized I never should have stopped her lessons at the studio. When I mentioned the possibility of studying again with your aunt, she broke down in tears."

"Oh, no. Poor Georgie."

"I only hope my past insults won't discourage Mrs. Gardiner from resuming my sister's lessons."

"Not to worry, William. I spoke with Aunt Maddy this morning, and she would like to do whatever she can to help Georgie get into the academy."

"Are you serious?" he asked, taken aback by this information.

"I am. In fact, my aunt plans to write a recommendation for your sister, and she would also like to help her prepare for the audition, if you have no objection."

"Objection?! Definitely not. In fact, I hardly know what to say. Your aunt is very generous."

"Yes, she is. Aunt Maddy thinks the academy will be an excellent place for Georgie."

William paused for a moment. "Liz, do you think Mrs. Gardiner would mind if I contacted her this weekend to make the arrangements?"

"Not at all."

"Good. I only wish I could speak with her in person. I don't like the idea of apologizing over the phone." He knitted his brows in frustration.

"I think you can put that frown away, Mr. Darcy," she playfully teased. "If you and Georgie are free tomorrow afternoon, your wish can be arranged."

"Tomorrow?"

"Yes. My aunt is having a very special gathering at her home on Sunday afternoon at three o'clock. When we spoke, she specifically asked me to invite you and Georgie."

"Why, I'd be more than happy to bring her. What's going on?"

"You of all people must have some insight into my aunt's affairs after your *investigation*." This time Elizabeth gave him a knowing look.

"Uh … yes, I might." He unconsciously tugged at the collar on his polo shirt, as if in some discomfort.

"Well, then are you aware that many notable musicians who perform with the Chicago Symphony often stay at the Gardiners' residence when they are in town?"

"No, I'm not."

"Aunt Maddy may live in Meryton Heights, but her house is worthy of the North Shore. She and Uncle Ed had it built after she retired from touring and took up teaching. Without giving away too many details, I have to tell you about one particular room at the rear of the house. My aunt worked with an architect to design a small recital hall which seats up to a hundred and fifty guests. With hardwood floors and a domed ceiling, the room is ideal for recording and giving chamber concerts. Then on an elevated stage, my aunt has placed two back-to-back concert grand pianos—a Steinway and Yamaha. Need I say more?"

"I'm impressed."

Speaking in a hushed tone, she continued, "This weekend a very famous Chinese pianist whose initials are L.L. is staying at the house *incognito* and has agreed to give a master class to one of our exceptional seniors from the academy. Can you guess who he is?"

William smiled. "I have a pretty good idea since I recently bought tickets to take Georgie to hear one such *virtuoso pianist* with the same initials this Monday night at Symphony Center."

"Our student was recently accepted by the Curtis Institute in New York where my aunt's guest went to school. She will be playing the first movement of the Beethoven *Appassionata*, which if I remember correctly, Georgie was studying before she stopped her lessons with Aunt Maddy. It's going to be a very exciting afternoon."

"I agree. Georgie will be beside herself when I tell her."

"If you two pick me up at my place around one o'clock, we should arrive early enough for you and Aunt Maddy to clear the air before the master class begins."

"I can't believe you arranged all of this. Liz, you are amazing."

"*Amazing?* You just keep on thinking that, Mr. Darcy," she teased. "Now if you don't mind, I'd like to speak with your sister."

"Sure, hold on, I'll get her. Thanks, Liz."

"No problem."

~ ♪ ~

10 December, Sunday
The Gardiner residence

The outing at Madeline Gardiner's House turned out to be exactly what Georgiana needed to be lifted out of her doldrums. Happy to see her former teacher, she was nearly in tears when they greeted one another. Georgiana wasted no time in making arrangements to resume her lessons in preparation for her audition at the music academy while William took the opportunity to apologize for his past behavior and unfounded accusations regarding the incident with George Wickham.

Not only did Georgiana delight in witnessing the skill of the world-renowned virtuoso pianist, but she also found a kindred spirit in the academy student, Ellen Masaki, who played with a musical sensitivity and maturity rarely found in a seventeen-year-old. Georgiana paid close attention when the maestro not only made suggestions, but also illustrated what he was trying to convey through demonstration. Following the master class, Mrs. Gardiner held an informal reception where spectators could ask questions of both student and teacher. Inspired by the events of the day, Georgiana eagerly sought out Ellen and the two of them formed an immediate friendship based on their mutual love of music. All in all, the afternoon proved to be an extraordinary experience for her.

~ ♪ ~

William's Car

"Oh, William," Georgiana gushed as soon as they were all situated in the car. "I never dreamed playing the piano could be so exciting. I think I have died and gone to heaven." Both William and Elizabeth chuckled at her enthusiasm. "Ellen Masaki was brilliant, but every time *HE* played, I got the shivers. His music spoke to me here." She clasped her hand to her breast. "I'm so inspired! I can't wait to get home and begin practicing for my lesson on Wednesday. Did you hear Ellen say she practices as much as *five hours a day?* And Mrs. Gardiner said once I am admitted to the academy, she'll place me in her advanced performance workshop along with Ellen, providing I work very hard. William, thank you *so* much for bringing me today."

"I can hardly take credit, Georgie, since it was Liz who arranged everything with her aunt."

"I'm so sorry, Miss Bennet. In my excitement, I didn't mean to sound ungrateful. How can we ever repay you?"

"Georgie, I don't expect anything in return. All I ask is that you work hard and take advantage of the wonderful opportunities you'll be given when you begin the academy next semester."

"I know I will, I promise." Georgiana sighed and leaned back into her seat, obviously reflecting over her afternoon.

Elizabeth and William continued making small talk about the master class and music in general with a few comments from Georgiana until they reached Elizabeth's apartment. Elizabeth had intended to invite the Darcys to come inside, but with Georgiana anxious to get home to begin practicing for her piano lesson, she decided to wait until another time. William did insist, however, on walking Elizabeth up to the front door of her building.

"Liz, I hardly know where to begin." He took her hands in his.

"This afternoon was a real turning point for Georgie, and it's all your doing."

"William, I didn't do anything … really. I merely had an inspiration and acted on it."

"Well, Miss Bennet." He reached up and gently touched her lips with his finger. "I have an inspiration which I'm dying to act on right now, but with my little sister watching from the car, I guess it will have to wait." He playfully wiggled his eyebrows in jest, causing her to giggle.

"Mr. Darcy, are you attempting to flirt with me?"

"It would seem so, Miss Bennet."

"Does this mean I can take a rain check?" She teasingly smiled and tilted her head in a way that made her appear very alluring.

"You can count on it. In the meantime, how about I call you later on tonight? I know you're pretty busy this week getting ready for the showcase, but if we can manage a late dinner during the week or plan something for the weekend, I'd really like to see you for a one-on-one."

"I'd love to." She beamed.

"Good, we'll talk soon." He gave Elizabeth a quick hug and kissed her cheek before leaving.

Watching them drive off, her hand involuntarily went to the place he had just kissed. "I'll be waiting, William," she whispered.

CHAPTER 6

FEEL THE JOY THAT'S IN THE AIR

Meryton Academy for the Performing Arts
Outside of the main office, Tuesday afternoon

"Elizabeth Bennet, what do you mean you're having dinner with William Darcy on Friday night? *And* he's *also* taking you to the gala? Wow! And here I thought you didn't even know the man. It *must* have been the dress." Elizabeth returned Charlotte's bra on Monday with the promise of buying a replacement, but they only now had a chance to discuss what had transpired since Bingley's party. At the time, nothing was said about one William Darcy or what had occurred between the two of them.

"Charlotte, don't even mention that dress. *Rent the Modern Closet* wasn't particularly happy when I told them what happened. Of course, in the end, they did offer me a free rental because of the mix-up. I'm thinking I'll cash it in for the gala. After all, it's going to be New Year's Eve, and I need a dress that will look great at the party. Plus, William plans to ask Skip if the band will play a *tango* for us. The man is incredible on the dance floor, by the way."

"The *tango?*" Charlotte slyly looked at Elizabeth. "If you ask me, I think *Billy* will be jealous."

"What are you talking about? I already told BC I'm not his date for the gala."

"If you say so. Although from what I heard in the teacher's lounge, he doesn't believe you actually have a date with the *all-important CEO of Darcy Enterprises*. He thinks you're just messing with him."

"Unbelievable!"

"Speaking of…. Here he comes now." Billy Collins was hurrying down the hallway, eagerly maneuvering his way between students while carrying an assortment of cables in one arm and a high-tech tool box in the other.

"Miss Bennet, Miss Bennet," he called somewhat out of breath as he approached the women. "May I please have a moment of your time? Nice to see you, Miss Lucas."

"Hey, Billy, what's up," Elizabeth casually responded.

"As you can see, I've just come from the Piano Lab. I replaced the faulty port on the console along with these two frayed connecting cables. You should have no problems in the foreseeable future."

"Thank you, Billy. You're a life-saver, and I appreciate your help." Her attention was suddenly drawn to the front doors, where William and Georgiana had entered. "Excuse me for a moment."

Greeting the Darcys, she quickly gave Georgiana a hug and asked them to meet two of her fellow colleagues. "Mr. William Darcy and Miss Georgiana Darcy, please allow me to present our resident dance instructor, Miss Charlotte Lucas, and one of our IT specialists, Mr. Billy Collins.

Before anyone could respond, Billy held out his hand to William saying, "William H. Collins the Second, at your service, sir." Firmly gripping William's hand as if to display his masculinity, he immediately offered, "*H* standing for Horatio—the proud name of my dear departed grandfather." He drew himself to his full height, although his eye only came level with William's chin.

William was a little surprised by the unusual manner of address, but having been forewarned by Elizabeth, he immediately responded with, "My pleasure, Mr. Collins." Then turning to Charlotte, he offered, "Miss Lucas, I have heard nothing but praise from Miss

Bennet with regards to your dance program here at the academy. Georgiana and I are looking forward to attending the December Showcase on Thursday."

"Thank you. I know you'll both enjoy it."

"Charlotte, Billy, please excuse us. The Darcys have an appointment with the dean at one o'clock, and I need to get to class."

As Elizabeth escorted the Darcys into the office, Charlotte leaned over to Billy, who was frowning with disdain at the familiarity between Elizabeth and William. "Give it up, Billy. She's with him."

The meeting with the dean of the academy went smoothly. The Darcys filled out the appropriate paperwork, Georgiana's transcripts were to be sent to the school, and the final audition for admission was scheduled during the second week in January.

As soon as the formalities were taken care of, Kitty was summoned to begin the official tour of the school, including the practice wing where the piano majors spent several hours a day. Kitty and Georgiana easily related to one another, and the trio enjoyed stopping by various classes—particularly Mrs. Gardiner's advanced piano performance workshop. The students were playing their recital pieces for one another and were encouraged to offer constructive criticism. Georgiana was introduced to the class as a prospective student and was warmly greeted by the piano majors, including Ellen Masaki, whom she had met on Sunday.

The final stop of the tour was at the auditorium where Elizabeth was rehearsing with the Vocalteens for their part in the showcase. Neither William nor Georgiana could believe how professional these students were, considering their ages. When William saw Elizabeth at work, he knew without a doubt he had made the right decision by encouraging his sister to apply. The caring atmosphere created by Elizabeth and so many other staff members who were dedicated to helping their students reach their potential was invigorating.

It's a holiday to remember, feel the joy that's in the air.
Once a year each December comes a magical time
When your spirits will climb,

A time to share, A time to give and a time to care
It's a holiday to remember
A season filled with love!

A Holiday to Remember – by Mac Huff

Watching the young people singing and dancing under Elizabeth's direction stirred something within William. Perhaps it was a little corny, but this was the first time since his parents died that he did feel the so-called *magic*. And he knew Georgiana felt it, too. It was all because of Elizabeth Bennet—a beautiful woman with a big heart, who somehow had captured his. This year, he vowed to do everything within his power to insure it was truly *A Holiday to Remember*.

~ ♪ ~

Late Thursday night following the showcase

"William!" Elizabeth exclaimed opening up the chat feature on her phone.

"It's not too late for you, is it?"

"No, not at all. It's always hard for me to unwind after my students perform. Right now, I'm sitting here with my chamomile tea watching a syrupy movie." She giggled. "It's called *A Holiday to Remember*, of all things. Can you believe it?"

"It must be fate." He chuckled.

"How did Georgie like the showcase? With so many parents wanting my attention, I hardly had a chance to speak with her."

"Need you ask? She wouldn't stop talking all the way home, and she was absolutely thrilled to meet your family. I figured Kitty must have told your mom about our parents. She's kind of a mother hen, isn't she?"

Elizabeth gave him a questioning look. "You mean to say my mother's *exuberance* didn't turn you off?"

"Not really. Aside from Richard's mother who comes by every now and then, my sister gets very little motherly attention. True, we do have our housekeeper, Mrs. Annesley, who is very competent, but she's not much of a mother figure. Your mom was so attentive, and Georgie loved it when she hugged her goodbye and invited her to come over on Saturday for the cookie bake."

"William...." Elizabeth tried not to giggle. "You have no idea what your sister has gotten into. By the time my mom is ready to release Georgie from her kitchen—she will *never* be the same. I wouldn't be surprised if you had a budding cookie chef on your hands when she gets back to your place. It's rather addicting."

"Thanks for the warning." He smiled.

"My younger sister, Lydia, who wasn't at the showcase, has also invited a couple of her friends, so I know Georgie will get lots of *girl time* as well. Lydia is a freshman and on the cheerleading squad at Meryton High. They had a basketball game tonight; otherwise you would have met her."

"Georgie will love it. Is there anything she can bring along to help out?"

"Are you kidding? My mom, *Cookie Baker Extraordinaire*, has *all* the bases covered. You name it—from Mexican Vanilla to Saigon Cinnamon to the world's finest chocolate—her baking cupboard is *never* empty. She and her many recruits have been baking cookies every Saturday for the last two months. In addition to the cookie exchange Mom organized at church, she also creates gift boxes filled with cookies to give to the elderly parishioners and our local nursing home. Not to mention her woman's circle probably supplies most of the military with cookies at the VA hospital where my sister Mary works as a physical therapist. Since you've offered to bring pizza for a bunch of hungry teenage bakers, I expect you're already on the list for your own gift box."

"I look forward to it. And trust me—they will not go to waste. Georgie and I plan to join Richard's family for a few days at Christmas in Northern Michigan. On his side of the family, there is an abundance of little cousins who will happily devour whatever we bring."

"Perfect!"

"Liz … I was wondering. While the cooks are heating up the kitchen on Saturday, would you be up for a little shopping? With Georgie resuming her lessons and looking forward to attending the academy, I would really like to buy her a better piano. I've browsed some on the internet, but truthfully, I haven't a clue what to look for."

"William, what a lovely thought. What is she playing on now?"

"She has a very good electric Yamaha, weighted keys and all, but I know it's not the same as playing on a real piano. My mom had an old Mason and Hamlin baby grand which, according to the piano tuner, wasn't worth restoring. Right now it's in storage along with a lot of other things belonging to my parents that we weren't ready to part with. Following their death, I sold our family home in Lake Forest, and Georgie and I permanently moved into my condo."

"Oh, Will…."

"Neither of us felt comfortable living there without our parents. There were just too many memories. She's never complained about the piano, but in hindsight, I probably should have gotten her a better instrument after the move."

"Not to worry. I have an idea!" Her eyes began to sparkle as her face took on that mischievous look which he had come to love. Do you have a certain price range in mind?"

"Liz, I'm not concerned about the price. I just want something of quality, a piano that will make Georgie happy and inspire her to practice."

"I think I know of something. Let me work on it tomorrow morning, and we'll talk more at dinner."

"You are the best. What would I do without you? Has it only been a week since Bingley's party?"

"Yes; seven crazy, busy, wonderful days to be precise." She beamed.

"Tell me, why is it I have the sudden urge to hold you in my arms and kiss you senseless?"

Her eyes went wide with the thought. "Why, Mr. Darcy … does this mean I can collect on another rain check in the very near future?"

"For certain, Miss Bennet. I'm making a mental note as we speak.

Well, I better let you go," he hesitantly said. "It may feel like the night is young, but my phone says it's already midnight."

"Midnight?" Her eyes sparkled, thinking of their first magical kiss.

"Liz?"

"It's nothing." She blushed. "I'm glad we got to talk. Goodnight, William. See you tomorrow."

"Tomorrow, Liz. Sweet dreams." He put his fingers to his lips and lightly touched the screen, prompting her to do the same.

"You too, Will."

CHAPTER 7

HOME IS WHERE THE HEART IS

Friday evening

The Friday night dinner date between William and Elizabeth was filled with great conversation and many stolen kisses. William took his special girl to an out-of-the-way restaurant in the suburbs called Antoinette's, where the food was excellent and the atmosphere was quiet. A violinist played romantic music in the background, and the couple enjoyed each other's company until the wee hours of the morning.

Reluctantly returning to Elizabeth's apartment, the two held hands as they walked into the building and took the elevator to the third floor. After another lingering kiss, William whispered, "Tell me, Liz Bennet, how did I ever manage to live without you?" He lovingly stroked her face.

She bit her lip and shyly smiled. "William, you make my head spin. There's nothing so very special about me. You've just been up in that high-rise office for too long and forgot how to have fun. I'm an ordinary girl from Meryton Heights who loves music and enjoys life. That's it."

"That *is* it. You enjoy life, and you've inspired me to try to do the same. As for the ordinary part ... not a chance. You are *anything* but ordinary." He kissed her again, crushing her to his chest before they parted. "You better get some sleep, Liz. I'll be here bright and early."

"Goodnight, William."

"Goodnight, Liz. Sweet dreams."

The next day

Even though William and Elizabeth got little sleep, the two were energized to begin their day. Arriving at the Bennet house close to nine in the morning, Elizabeth could see her mother eagerly watching out the window for her newest baker. On entering, she immediately pulled Georgiana into a tight hug. "My sweet child, please come in out of the cold. Kitty and Lydia are in the kitchen making hot chocolate, and Lydia's friends should be arriving anytime now. Lizzy, you and William go on ahead and leave Georgie to me. She'll be in good hands." Mrs. Bennet took her coat and hung it in the hall closet, leaving Georgiana speechless. In addition to the matriarch's motherly affection, the interior of the Bennet house looked like something out of a storybook. Mrs. Bennet was not only an avid cookie baker, but also a true crafter at heart, filling nearly every corner, nook and cranny in her house with what she called *personalized necessities*.

Leaving the house, Elizabeth leaned into William, saying, "I do hope you realize that if Georgie shows the slightest interest in any of my mother's hobbies, your home will never look the same. Mom is more than willing to share her *little pleasures* in life and will gladly indoctrinate your sister into making things for her favorite charities, as well as your condo."

"Liz, if sharing in your mother's hobbies makes Georgie happy, then I'll look forward to it. She's missed so much with my parents gone."

"You're a good man, William. And ... if you happen to have any regrets down the road, I'll be happy to remind you of what you just said. Let's see what your decoupage and tatted doilies tolerance level is." William rolled his eyes in mock protest as the two broke into laughter.

Fifteen minutes later, William and Elizabeth arrived at Mrs. Gardiners' house. From there they traveled to an address on the south side of Chicago in Hyde Park, near the University of Chicago. The Steinway piano they were going to view belonged to an elderly woman, Mrs. Anna Boynton, who happened to be Madeline Gardiner's first piano teacher.

"I know both of you will enjoy meeting my old teacher," said Mrs. Gardiner. "Anna taught many aspiring young professional artists in her day, several of whom have enjoyed long concert careers. The Steinway was built in 1913. I recently played the instrument and found the tone in the upper range to be vibrant and bright while the lower range is deep and resonant. Having taught Georgiana and knowing what type of music she favors, I think this instrument would be ideal for her studies."

"What's the price of the piano, if you don't mind me asking?" William curiously inquired.

"Ah yes, the price. Well, Anna is donating the profits from the sale of the piano to our scholarship fund at the academy and is hoping the instrument will be purchased for one of our students. As to the actual dollar amount, Anna is requesting the purchaser to remit fifteen thousand dollars—the same price she paid to have the instrument restored. After playing the piano, however, I know it's worth far more. I checked with the technician who did the restoration, and he told me the Steinway could easily sell for thirty-five thousand dollars. If you like the piano, we can arrange another appointment with Anna and bring Georgiana in to try it out before completing the transaction."

"This sounds very doable, and I look forward to seeing the piano and hearing you play. Mrs. Gardiner, once again, please let me apologize for my foolishness. Your kindness towards my sister is humbling."

"Mr. Darcy, all of us have made mistakes and hopefully have learned from our shortcomings. Georgiana is a lovely, talented young lady, and I am more than happy to assist both of you."

"Thank you."

Mrs. Boynton's home was well cared for, and the elderly woman had a companion who saw to her needs. Following introductions and a cup of tea, Mrs. Boynton proceeded to interview William about his sister. Aside from Mrs. Gardiner's recommendation, she wished to know Georgiana's background and more about her desire to play the piano. Once she was satisfied, she asked Mrs. Gardiner to sit at the keyboard and play a sampling of several styles, allowing William and Elizabeth to hear the versatility of the instrument. As expected, they were thrilled with the sound of the Steinway, and William had no qualms about completing the transaction.

"Mrs. Boynton," remarked William following Mrs. Gardiner's demonstration, "your piano is superb, and I would be honored to purchase it on my sister's behalf. You can rest assured this instrument will receive a welcoming home."

Before departing, William and Elizabeth agreed to bring Georgiana to visit Mrs. Boynton on the following Tuesday so she could play the piano herself and meet the elderly woman before finalizing the purchase. Unbeknownst to the others, William also decided he would anonymously donate the full value of the piano to the scholarship fund, following Georgiana's official acceptance to the academy. In his opinion, she would be gaining far more than an education by playing this piano and attending the academy, and he could not put a price on his sister's happiness.

~ ♪ ~

By the time William and Elizabeth returned to the Bennet house with pizza, the bakers had been on a sugar-high for quite some time. Mrs. Bennet was definitely in her *element*, joyfully overseeing the baking and interacting with the energetic teenagers. Elizabeth quietly chuckled to herself and gave William a knowing look as she watched his reaction.

"William!" Georgiana exclaimed. "Just look at how many boxes we put together for the shut-ins at Mrs. Bennet's church. Plus these are for Mary to take to the VA hospital on Monday! Not to mention these other boxes are for us to take when we go to Michigan. Every box has at least six or seven varieties of cookies. I never dreamed cookie baking could be so much fun!"

"I'm impressed," Darcy answered sampling one of the cookies on the plate. "This is delicious!" he exclaimed while reaching for another. The plate was filled with everything from traditional sugar cookies to Peppermint Pattie-stuffed chocolate cookies, gingerbread, thumbprint cookies with an assortment of fillings, peanut butter balls and finally oatmeal raisin. "And all of you still have room for pizza?"

"Yes!" was the overwhelming response.

It was at least another hour before the pizza was devoured and Georgiana was ready to leave. Before departing, Mrs. Bennet cornered William to put in yet another request. "William, since the holiday season is practically upon us, I wonder if you and Georgie might be able to join us tomorrow night for a progressive dinner party. It's nothing too elaborate and only involves a few of my friends from church. We start off at the Longs for Cocktails and hors d'oeuvres. From there we all gather at the Phillips' for Soup and salad. The Mitchells will be serving the Entrée and then we finish here for dessert." With Mrs. Bennet having discovered William's interest in her Lizzy, she felt this would be the perfect time to help further their relationship. In Franny Bennet's mind, food and fellowship was all about love, family and tradition. With the Darcys having very little immediate family in their lives, it was only natural that they now become a part of hers.

As it turned out Mrs. Bennet's invitation was only the beginning of a very full week. Following the progressive dinner, William invited the younger girls to join him and Elizabeth for an evening at the Chicago Botanic Gardens where they delighted in an old fashioned sleigh ride and a tour of the festival of lights. Then at Georgiana's suggestion, they all enjoyed one final outing before the week was over. This time it was to Millennium Park for an afternoon of ice-skating followed by dim sum in Chinatown. After all was said and done, the two youngest Bennet girls and Georgiana had bonded as best friends and planned to get together several more times during the holiday break.

"Oh, William," Georgiana sighed after they dropped the girls off and took Elizabeth home. "This has been one of the best weeks I've ever had. The Bennets are like family and I love them all so much. And more importantly ... I love you."

"Georgie." He squeezed her hand. "I love you too, sweetheart."

"Of course nothing can compare with my new piano. I keep remembering Mrs. Boynton and how proud she was to have me play it. William, I never dreamed I would have the chance to play such a beautiful instrument. I promise you will *never* regret buying the piano for me and I shall always treasure it."

"I know you will. Our mother would have been pleased."

William couldn't help smiling as they drove back to his condo. He had wanted this holiday season to be special for Georgiana, and it was. And because he had Elizabeth in his life, this season had also become very special for him.

~ ♫ ~

Elizabeth's apartment
Friday evening, 22 December

Elizabeth buzzed the front door open as she called through the intercom, "Come on up, William. Maybe you should take the stairs instead of the elevator and burn a few calories since I have enough food to feed an army."

"Will do—be right there." This was the first time Elizabeth had invited William to her apartment. As he climbed the stairs, he couldn't help but remember the Bennet residence where a multitude of crafts and holiday decorations seemed to engulf the entire house. For a brief moment he wondered if Elizabeth was anything like her mother in that respect. Recalling how she had playfully jested about Mrs. Bennet's obsession, the thought was quickly dismissed. When William got to the top of the stairs, he suddenly stopped, fascinated by the vision which greeted him. There stood Elizabeth wiping her hands on a flour smudged apron. Yet that was not what made him hold his breath. His eyes were immediately drawn to her gorgeous long legs and her ruby-red stiletto heels, tempting him from beneath what appeared to be a very flattering little black dress.

"Don't mind me," she said, quickly untying the apron and releasing the clip which held her long hair. "I was just cleaning up after putting an apple pie in the oven. Everything else is pretty much ready to go."

"Did you say apple pie?" His eyes lit up and without further hesitation, he strode forward and kissed Elizabeth on the cheek before handing her a bouquet of red roses and holding up the bottle of wine he brought for the occasion.

"That I did," she exclaimed, inhaling deeply." I love roses! They're beautiful. Come on in." She gave him a quick kiss and led him into the living room.

"I can't remember when I last had homemade apple pie. You definitely know the way to a man's heart, Miss Bennet." He made a dramatic gesture clasping his hand to his chest. "Granny Smith?"

"Lodi. They taste way better than Grannies but are only in season for about three weeks in the summer. I always buy a bushel at the farmers' market and freeze half in case a hungry man with a hollow leg comes along and is in need of an all-American favorite," she teased. Elizabeth was convinced William had a high metabolism since he could eat circles around her and didn't seem to have an ounce of fat on his lean, hard body.

William placed the bottle of wine on the table and trailed her into the kitchen where he watched as she took a vase out of the cupboard and readied it for the flowers.

"I could never compete with my mother when it comes to making desserts, but in this case, I'm known as the *apple pie queen.*"

"Apple pie is one of my all-time favorites, and it smells delicious. So what else have you got planned?"

"Other than the pie, there's really nothing too fancy on the menu." She led him back out of the kitchen and placed the flowers in the center of the dining room table. "Jane is considered the *gourmet cook* in our family and is always searching for a new dish to serve. Her kitchen is loaded with cook books and we rarely eat the same thing twice when we dine at her place. In general, my cooking skills follow the basics, although I do like to experiment with various spices and marinades. In my opinion, cooking is all about *flavor*."

"I think I can handle the basics," he said, taking her hand and pulling her close for a long kiss. "Speaking of flavor," he said after breaking the kiss, "you taste delicious—apples and cinnamon at their best."

She licked her lips and smiled. "You should know a good cook always samples her wares as she's working away in the kitchen. Come on." She took his hand. "Let me finish showing you around my humble abode while we're waiting."

Elizabeth's one-bedroom apartment wasn't particularly large, but it was homey. The hardwood floors and baseboards combined with some Cherrywood antiques and a few handmade quilts once belonging to Grandmother Bennet gave her place a bit of a country look. She chose light and airy colors, and a scenic watercolor of birch trees lining a winding dirt road hung over the mantelpiece above the gas fireplace.

"I bought the painting from a local artist in Door County, Wisconsin when Char and I went there a couple of years ago. Have you ever been?"

"No, I haven't. Although I've heard it's a beautiful area to visit, rustic and what-not."

"It is, even though most villages cater to tourists. I think it's well worth making the trip at least once to escape the city during the summer. Char and I only went as far north as Sister Bay, but there are interesting places to stop all along the peninsula. I can't begin to tell you how many eclectic museums and little art galleries we visited, not to mention there are loads of places for hiking as well as water sports if you like that type of thing. Then if you're looking for unusual gifts, the local shops are awesome. And the food! *So* delicious. Here, let me show you. I still have a few pictures from our trip." Elizabeth picked up her phone and began scrolling through her gallery until she found what she was looking for.

"Beautiful!"

"Both of these pictures are from Peninsula State Park. Char and I picnicked there and did some serious hiking before we came home. The park isn't far from Sister Bay where there is a wonderful music store which carries all sorts of ethnic folk instruments. Look here. This Celtic Folk Harp is one of my favorite finds, and I'm thinking of buying one on my next trip—that is if I can figure out how to get it home. If you remember, my Cavalier is pretty small."

"How could I forget?" He chuckled. "Do you think you can find a place for it? It's already pretty cozy in here."

"It'll be tight, but I thought I could squeeze it in over there by the window if I move a few plants back into my office and put the rocking chair in my bedroom. If not, I can always take it to school."

"Sounds good to me." He nodded.

"I also thought I might pick up a few more instruments for school when I go again. Last time, I purchased a hand-crafted dulcimer. I'd show it to you now, but it's in my office at the academy. One of my students figured out how to play it and is working up an arrangement for a medley of Appalachian folksongs I'm putting together for our Spring Showcase. One song in particular tells a beautiful story of unrequited love. Charlotte is going to choreograph it in modern dance for Kitty and a couple of her other students to act out while my choir is singing. With the right lighting, I think it's going to be one of the highlights of our showcase."

"Liz, I'm amazed at all you do—in awe, actually. The creative forces coming from the academy are beyond what I first imagined when you mentioned the school. Georgie's going to love it."

"I'm sure she will. Say, do you think that the two of you would like to join me when I go up to Door County again?"

"I'm up for it, and Richard has a truck we could borrow if you want to purchase the harp and bring it back when we go."

"That would be fantastic!"

"We could make a long weekend of it, or even take a full week after school lets out in June. I haven't taken a real vacation in ages."

"Why am I not surprised?" Elizabeth giggled as he defensively shrugged his shoulders.

"Then Door County it is!" Elizabeth put down her phone and took William's hand leading him back through the kitchen and out into an enclosed sunporch which she had converted to her office and music room. "This is the last of the tour. What do you think?"

With windows on three sides, William imagined the room to be very cheery in the daylight hours. Elizabeth obviously loved plants and had several hanging from the ceiling and a few others settled on the windowsills. Along the main wall, she had positioned her keyboard and computer for working at home and in the corner next to a lounge chair, there was a cozy drum table where she ate breakfast. "This place suits you," William remarked. "I like it very much."

Walking back into the dining room, Elizabeth asked William to pour the wine, and they sat on the couch while they waited for the pie to finish. She talked some about her family, and William told her a little more about the trip he and Georgiana were about to take on the next day. Richard's brother owned a small house used for family gatherings near a ski resort in the upper peninsula of Michigan.

"Every year our extended family joins the Fitzwilliams for some family time and outdoor adventures over the Christmas weekend. I can't say I'm much into skiing or snowboarding, but it's a nice change of pace," William offered. "After my parents died, the holidays were so dismal." Elizabeth snuggled in a little closer, offering him comfort as she listened.

"The first year they were gone was the worst. The anticipation of every holiday, anniversary or anything holding a fond memory seemed to prey on our emotions. At the time, letting Georgie spend a few days with her cousins instead of moping around the condo turned out to be the best medicine for both of us. This will be our third year going. Richard is no longer married, but he still brings his two girls, who are only a little younger than Georgie. I don't suppose you happen to ski or snowboard?"

"I'm sorry to disappoint you, William." She sat up tall. "The only time I ever went skiing was when I was a freshman in college. My family was visiting relatives in Milwaukee, and if a true confession must be made, my greatest feat was basically gliding down *Chicken Ridge* without falling." They both chuckled. "On the other hand, I really did like ice-skating the other day at Millennium Park. Maybe, sometime you and I should go back … *without* our sisters. I hear it's very romantic in the evenings, Mr. Darcy." Her eyes sparkled as she looked into his.

"Romantic…." He stroked her cheek. "Liz…." Before she knew it, William had pulled her onto his lap and held her close. Their kisses were filled with passion, and it wasn't long before they were stretched out on the couch—legs and arms entwined with one another. The two barely came up for air and didn't stop kissing until the timer on the stove went off, awakening them from their desires.

"Uh oh!" Elizabeth giggled, breaking their embrace and quickly sitting up. "Excuse me, Mr. Darcy, but *that* little reminder is your apple pie." She stood up, pulled her hair back and straightened her dress. "Come with me, William." She grabbed his hand. "I think I better put you to work. It's time you earned your keep! For the next hour, there will be *no* distracting the cook."

"Yes, ma'am," he said before pulling her back into his arms for one more kiss. A few seconds later, the timer beeped again prompting him to say, "Okay! I surrender!"

True to her word, Elizabeth put William directly to work sautéing mushrooms and onions. While he stood over the frying pan, she turned on the broiler and took out the steaks which had been marinating in her special sauce where the secret ingredient was beer. "I don't actually drink beer, but I love cooking with it. It's a great tenderizer and seems to improve the flavor of the meat. I also added fresh ginger root, minced garlic, and hot pepper, followed by sesame oil, soy sauce and a little corn starch for thickening. I promise you are going to love the combination."

"I'm practically salivating in anticipation."

"Hold that thought." Elizabeth had also fixed twice baked potatoes, asparagus, fresh tomato-basil salad and homemade bread. A little reheating was all that was required while the meat was broiling. After finishing dinner and enjoying the apple pie, the two were so full that they struggled to put away the leftovers and load the dishwasher.

The couch was beginning to look very tempting, and the two lovers opted for some serious cuddling to the tune of *It's a Wonderful Life* showing on one of the movie channels. Elizabeth and William felt so comfortable with one another that somewhere during the middle of the movie they both drifted off to sleep and didn't wake up until they heard the closing refrains of *Auld Lang Syne* being sung.

Checking the mantle clock Elizabeth spoke softly, "William, it's midnight. You've got to get going. Morning will be here before you know it, and you and Georgie have a long drive tomorrow."

"Midnight," he sighed pulling her closer and placing soft kisses on her neck and face until he finally secured her mouth in one last heated kiss. "What if I told you I didn't want to leave?"

"Oh, Will…."

"I can't leave." He tenderly looked at her. "Not at least until I've told you how much I love you, Elizabeth Bennet."

"You love me?"

"With all my heart. Liz, being with you makes me feel like a different person. I know I'm sounding like one of those crazy characters from your favorite movie channel, but when I'm with you, I really do feel like I've come home."

"Me too, William. I love you so very much. The first time you kissed me was *magical,* and from that moment, my feelings have only grown stronger." Again they kissed.

"So, Liz, does this mean you're my girl now?"

"Yes, William, I am definitely yours."

CHAPTER 8

THE PEMBERLEY FOUNDATION GALA

Elizabeth's apartment
New Year's Eve

*E*lizabeth stood in front of the mirror in her bedroom admiring the beautiful ruby pendant William had given her just one week after declaring their love for one another. *"The ruby is the gem of the heart,"* he had said. *"And since you hold my heart, I want you to wear this for me."* Thus far, Elizabeth had worn it every day. She loved what the necklace symbolized, and more importantly, the dear man who gave it to her. "William," she murmured.

Earlier in the day, William had dropped Georgiana off at the Bennets' for a sleepover with Kitty and Lydia to welcome in the New Year. From there, he picked up Elizabeth and drove north to Forest Ridge Country Club where Billy and Skip were already setting up the cables and equipment for the sound system to be used by her choral group and the band. After speaking with Mr. Reynolds, Elizabeth wondered if the staging area might be a little tight to accommodate the dance moves which were a part of the holiday medley. If need be, she could make a few adjustments at the last minute as long as she knew what to expect.

The country club itself was a posh private organization located adjacent to Lake Michigan, a little north of the Chicago Botanic Gardens and the Ravinia Summer Festival Music Park. The entrance to the club was hidden in a forested area with winding roads leading back to the main buildings, tennis courts and golf course. At this time of year, the winter gardens were scenic, and the trees surrounding the club house were adorned with tiny sparkling lights. The entire setting was inviting like something out of a fairy-tale—perfect for a winter wedding.

"Wedding!" Elizabeth's eyes widened, and her face flushed with the thought. "I can't believe I'm thinking of weddings when I've only been with him for a little over three weeks—not even a full month." She giggled. "Now I know I've been watching way too many holiday movies!" Again she giggled.

How could one man have become so integral to her life in such a short time? She felt giddy with the thought. Some might think she was acting like a teenager who had a schoolgirl crush, but for Elizabeth, her feelings ran far deeper. In her mind, she and William Darcy were soulmates, and words could not begin to describe the bond which existed between them.

Having finished with her hair and makeup, she reached for her free rental from *Rent the Modern Closet,* took it out of the dress bag and held it up in front of the long mirror on her closet door. The burgundy red chiffon fabric shimmered. Waves of tiny sequins decorated the strapless sweetheart bodice, which was intricately ruched and cinched with a twist at the waist. This dress was far more elegant than the one she had worn to Bingley's party, and it was one she wouldn't be embarrassed to wear in front of her students. Yet with the discreet side slit, it would be perfect for dancing the tango with William.

All at once, Elizabeth was startled from her musings by the sound of the buzzer announcing William's arrival downstairs. "Oh no! He's here, and I don't even have my dress on!" Panicking, she rushed to the intercom and buzzed him in. "Come on up, William. The door's unlocked. I'm still getting dressed."

"Be right up, beautiful!"

Hurrying back to her room, Elizabeth picked up the dress, unzipped it and slithered in. It was a tight squeeze with a narrow zipper opening, but she managed to wiggle in and pulled the strapless bodice into place. As soon as she pulled up the zipper and slipped on her shoes, she would be ready to greet William.

"You've got to be kidding! The darn thing is stuck!" She arched her back while trying to free the zipper. "Ouch!" Not only was the fabric caught in the zipper, but now, so were a few strands of her long hair. No matter how much she tugged, the zipper wouldn't budge, and with her hair caught as well, she couldn't twist the dress around to where she could see how to fix it.

"Liz, I'm here."

"Oh, William, I'm having the worst time with my dress. I'm so sorry, but I really need your help. Could you please come in the bedroom?" Holding the bodice to her chest and with her head bent to one side she self-consciously turned to face him. "The zipper's caught."

"Darcy to the rescue," he said walking into her room. "Here, let me see what I can do." She turned around. "I see the problem. It looks easy enough to pull your hair free, but the zipper may prove harder—it has a mouthful of fabric."

"Do what you can. If I ruin another dress, *Rent the Modern Closet* will have my head."

"Not if I can help it. Hold still, Liz."

With one yank, William was able to pull her hair free. "Oh, that's so much better. I owe you." She turned her head and gave him a quick kiss. "Now, see if you can ease the fabric out by wiggling the zipper up and down. Be careful. It's chiffon and can easily snag."

"Got it."

Elizabeth felt one of William's warm hands slip inside of her dress and grab the fabric around the zipper while the other hand began working on the slider. His touch against her bare back was nearly her undoing, and it became obvious that it was his, too, when he momentarily stopped and tenderly kissed her bare shoulder. "William?"

"Sweetheart, I'm not sure how long my resolve will hold in this tempting situation."

"William, please, you have to stay focused. We have a party to attend."

"Yes, ma'am." William couldn't resist kissing her shoulder once more before starting in again on the zipper. "It won't be long, Liz, I almost have it."

"Good!"

"There! Mission accomplished!" William carefully finished zipping the zipper. "Now, turn around and let me have a look." He stepped back. "Liz, you take my breath away," he nearly whispered. Gently touching the ruby pendant, he lifted his fingers to caress her cheek. "I love you," he said sealing his vow with a kiss.

"I love you, too, William."

"I brought something for you." He took her hand and led her into the living room. Opening a medium-sized flower box, he presented Elizabeth with a wrist corsage.

"Gardenias! Oh, William, I absolutely love the smell." She inhaled deeply.

"There's one more under the tissue. I asked the florist to attach one of the flowers to a hair clip. If it seems like too much, you needn't wear it."

"No, not at all. It's beautiful."

"May I?" She nodded. William carefully smoothed her long hair behind her left ear and clipped the flower in place. "They say that when a woman wears a flower in this manner, it means she is taken."

"William Darcy, I'm yours, without question, just as *you* are mine." Again they kissed. Moments later, William helped Elizabeth with her wrap. They headed down to the car and drove directly to Forest Ridge in anticipation of a lovely evening while attending the gala and welcoming in the New Year.

~ ♪ ~

Forest Ridge Country Club

William and Elizabeth arrived at the country club close to six o'clock. Although dinner wasn't scheduled to start until seven, the ballroom was beginning to fill with guests who were either lined up at the bar or milling about in conversation before taking their seats. After checking their coats, William happily introduced Elizabeth to several of his associates who were on the board of the foundation.

A little later, the couple happened to notice Richard's arrival with Caroline clinging to his arm. Dressed in a form-fitting mermaid dress and adorned with an excessive amount of gold jewelry, Caroline literally teetered as she walked across the floor with her escort. She held herself tall, surreptitiously looking around the room as if to check who might be paying her notice.

"William, is that really Caroline Bingley? Dressed like something out of Fredrick's of Hollywood?" Liz asked in disbelief.

"I'm afraid so. When I told Richard about us, he offered to run interference with her at tonight's event. The man is far braver than I thought. Here they come."

"William," Caroline simpered, refusing to acknowledge Elizabeth's presence. "What a shame I was unable to accept your invitation for this evening."

"I never…."

"Richard *insisted* I accompany him tonight, didn't you, darling?" she cooed, leaning into her date as he rolled his eyes. "Don't you worry, William. With Eliza no doubt playing *musical diva* tonight, I'm sure we'll have *plenty* of time to catch up, if you know what I mean." She disgustingly parted her lips and moistened them with the tip of her tongue.

William was appalled by her inference, especially with Elizabeth standing beside him. Before he could make his mind known, Richard interrupted Caroline's little exhibition. "Excuse me, William, Liz. I believe *Caroline* is in want of some refreshments, aren't you, my dear?" He glared at the woman and not too subtly took her by the arm, directing her towards the bar. Her shrill laughter was unnerving as they walked away.

"My goodness! Does she always act like that?" Elizabeth asked, rather stunned.

"For as long as I can remember ... pretty much, yes. Hopefully Richard can keep her in line. Regardless, you are with me tonight, and I don't plan to let you out of my sight for one minute." He tenderly kissed her.

"Thank you, William. I think I'll rather enjoy having you for my protector." She smiled sweetly.

"Good. I see a few more people I'd like you to meet before dinner. Shall we?"

The rest of the cocktail hour proved to be uneventful. Promptly at seven, just as dinner was about to be served, Bob Reynolds stepped up to the microphone in the staging area, introducing himself and making announcements about the silent auction and entertainment taking place during the course of the evening. Following his brief speech, William was introduced and handed the microphone.

"Happy New Year!" he greeted. "I would like to take this opportunity to welcome you to our New Year's Eve Pemberley Foundation Gala. Once again, we come together to raise money as a presenting partner for MADD, *Mothers Against Drunk Driving*. Exactly four years ago tonight Darcy Enterprises lost James Darcy, its CEO and founder of the Pemberley Foundation Charities, along with his wife Anne to a drunk driver. Since that time, this foundation has raised more than one million dollars through private donations and events such as tonight's gala for the MADD organization. As many of you know, in addition to this evening's fundraiser, our foundation supports more than twenty other charities in the Chicago metropolitan area. On behalf of my family, Darcy Enterprises, and the Pemberley Foundation, I thank all of you for your continued support and wish you a very enjoyable evening."

The catered dinner at the country club was a beautiful affair and went off smoothly. Around eight o'clock, about the time dessert was being served, William and Elizabeth excused themselves to welcome the Vocalteens and the accompanying parents who were waiting in an adjoining room off to the side. Greeting the performers and their guests, William expressed his pleasure in presenting such a talented group of young people at the foundation's gala. He invited all of them to stay on for dessert once their performance was finished. William proudly watched as Elizabeth lined up her students and led them through a few vocal warm-ups before giving some final instructions about the setup and a few adjustments they might need to make once they were on the stage.

Billy Collins, now knowing he had no chance with Elizabeth, made one valiant attempt to apologize. On the pretext of discussing something about the sound system, he cornered Elizabeth with his prepared speech. "Miss Bennet, I realized earlier today I was mistaken in assuming I would be your … ahem, date this evening. I would never have presumed such a thing on your part had you not asked me to run sound for the choir. Miss Lucas attempted to point out my error, but I did not give her warning credence. Forgive me if I have caused you any undo distress."

"Billy, I'm so sorry you misunderstood. Please allow me to say how much I truly appreciate all you are doing to assist with our performance tonight." She gave him a quick kiss on the cheek, causing the man to puff out his chest and smile with great pleasure. "Now, what do you say we *get the show on the road?*" He politely nodded and went directly to the sound table.

When it was time for the Vocalteens to perform, Elizabeth graciously introduced her students, telling the audience a little about the music academy and the medley they were about to perform. To make things easier, she had prepared pre-recorded instrumental tracts to be used during their performance. As soon as Elizabeth signaled Billy, he cued up the music, and *A Holiday to Remember* began.

The Vocalteens were very professional and full of energy. At the close the audience rose to a standing ovation in appreciation. After the students left the stage and reassembled in the adjoining room for dessert, Mr. Reynolds, William and several other supporters followed them and offered their congratulations. Elizabeth could not have been prouder of her choir and was pleased they had been able to support the gala with their outstanding talent in this small way.

Once the choir and their parents departed, it was nine-thirty and the party was well underway. Although the band had been playing for some time, Elizabeth's set wasn't scheduled for another hour. Just before going on, she turned to William and whispered, "How's your Spanish?"

"Enough to get by."

"Good, because the last song I'll be singing tonight is for you, Mr. Darcy." Her smile was beguiling and after giving him a quick kiss, she ascended the stairs to the stage and took the mic in hand. The musical set was filled with old romantic standards which were perfectly suited to Elizabeth's voice. William was seated at a table a little off to the side where he could easily watch Elizabeth while intermittently chatting with a few friends. Every so often, she turned his way and flashed him one of her tempting smiles. By the time Elizabeth got to *his* song, he was no longer attentive to any conversation whatsoever, as he was completely captivated by the one woman who held his heart. The song was hypnotic and filled with longing. Her silky voice was nearly his undoing when she sang *Bésame, Bésame Mucho—Kiss me, Kiss me again*, written in 1940 by Consuelo Velázquez.

Once Elizabeth stepped down from the stage, she was enthusiastically besieged by several of the guests who raved about her performance with the band and wanted her attention. William, however, had a very different idea, and all he needed was to see her mischievous smile before setting his plan in motion.

"Miss Bennet, your performance was outstanding. I congratulate you," he said displaying an engaging smile of his own.

"Thank you, Mr. Darcy. It was my great pleasure to sing in honor of the foundation this evening."

"Might I have a word?" She nodded. "Please excuse us," he said to the remaining well-wishers and stepped forward to claim her hand. From there, he discreetly led her through the crowd until they were able to exit the ballroom and enter the room previously occupied by her students. The room had since been cleared and the lights were dim. Shutting the door, he immediately pulled her into his arms and whispered the words she had just sung in Spanish. *"Kiss me, kiss me as if tonight was the last time."* The longing and desire which they had both been feeling suddenly exploded into a passion of fiery kisses and caresses. For the two lovers, time seemed to stand still, and nothing else mattered but their need for one another.

Finally breaking apart, they continued to stare into each other's eyes, not wanting the magic of this special time to end. To their great pleasure, the band resumed playing. This time it was a slow Latin dance—perfectly suited to the tango. Without saying a word, William extended his hand. He led Elizabeth to the middle of the room where they began the sensuous dance with an embrace. Mirroring each other, they took the appropriate pose required by the opening of the dance, and following William's lead, the two began. They stepped, they rocked, and they glided, turning only to begin again. As their steps became bolder and more elaborate, they continued to move as one, never losing sight of each other. Like a drug, the connection building between the two was all consuming. When the dance came to a close, William crushed Elizabeth to his chest and held her tightly within his embrace as he tried to rein in his ardor. "My darling girl," he whispered into her hair—his voice husky and his breath ragged. "That was exquisite."

"William…." She looked into his eyes, feeling much as he did.

"After dancing with you I fully understand why my parents loved this particular dance so much." Again they kissed. "Liz…." He forced himself to release her from his embrace and simply held her hands. "As much as I wish to stay here like this for the rest of the evening, we probably should get back to the party before we're missed."

"I know. Can you imagine what your staff would say if one of them caught their CEO and his girlfriend sneaking in here to make out like a couple of teenagers?"

He groaned. "Yes, I can. And if Richard didn't have Caroline to contend with, we probably would have been found out within minutes of making our escape to this room. Believe me—I would never hear the end of it."

"Well, then, Mr. Darcy," she teased, "It seems we owe *Miss Bingley* a debt of gratitude this evening."

"I wouldn't go quite that far, Miss Bennet." They chuckled. "Let's return to the party, and if you have no objection, we can come back here to watch the fireworks from the windows and greet the New Year at midnight."

"*Midnight?*" She beamed.

"Yes, midnight."

Walking hand in hand, the couple made their way back into the main ballroom, where apparently they hadn't been missed by anyone with the exception of Caroline. The woman nearly exploded when she figured out where they had been and speculated about what they had been doing.

"Will you just look at the two of them? I think I might gag."

"Caroline," Richard chided. "*Jealousy* does *not* become you."

"She has no right to William. I've been working on the man for a solid two years now," she nearly spat.

"Let it go, Caroline. You're wasting your time on Darcy." He leaned in close and whispered in her ear, "You know, Caro, you're actually a pretty fun date when you're not obsessing over William. How about we get out of here and head down to the city. The roads are clear. We could be on the expressway in no time and take in one of the late-night clubs on Rush Street."

She smiled seductively, "Okay, Richard, let's see if you can show me a good time."

Shortly before midnight, the guests either gathered at the east windows of the ballroom or braved the cold out on the terrace to watch the fireworks and greet the New Year. William and Elizabeth quietly slipped back into their hideaway, which was still unoccupied. With his arms wrapped around her waist, the two stood together by the windows, looking out over Lake Michigan as it shimmered beneath the reflection of the moon. Within moments, the first of the fireworks were set off, signaling midnight and the beginning of a New Year. As soon as the band began playing *Auld Lang Syne,* William turned Elizabeth in his arms and whispered, "Happy New Year, Liz."

"Happy New Year, William." Their kiss was not only filled with passion, but with commitment and promise of what was to come.

"Liz," William tenderly said with his heart full of love. "Liz, I love you so much. I realize we haven't been together for very long, but I feel with every fiber of my being this is where we belong. In my heart, I know we were meant to be, and I can't imagine spending the rest of my life with anyone but you." Taking her hands in his, he knelt before her and asked, "Elizabeth Bennet, my darling Liz, will you marry me?"

"Oh, Will...." She dropped in front of him and said with tears forming in her eyes, "I want nothing more than to be your wife. Yes ... yes, I will marry you with all of my heart." Embracing, they sealed their pledge with a tender kiss.

Pulling Elizabeth to her feet, William brushed aside the tears which had moistened her cheeks saying, "When I bought your necklace, I couldn't help but make a second purchase." Her eyes grew wide as he reached into his pocket and took out a small box. Opening it, he presented Elizabeth with the most elegant marquise-cut two-carat solitaire engagement ring and lovingly placed it on her finger.

"William, I'm ... oh my gosh," she said, with tears slipping once more from the corners of her eyes. "It's ... it's beautiful. Oh, William, I love you so."

Again he wiped her tears, and after gently kissing her hand, pulled her into his embrace. "Sweetheart, this ring is merely a reflection of the treasure I'm holding right here in my arms. Elizabeth Bennet, you are more beautiful and more precious to me than any jewel I could ever hope to buy."

New Year's Day

When William and Elizabeth finally left the party, it was long past two in the morning. There were farewells and words of appreciation to be shared with those who were in attendance, not to mention the interaction with dozens of guests who offered up their congratulations after seeing Elizabeth's beautiful engagement ring. Jane was beside herself with joy, and Bingley confided to William his thoughts had been going along those same lines, though perhaps not quite as impetuously.

With all of the excitement surrounding their engagement, neither William nor Elizabeth felt the least bit tired. Instead of taking Elizabeth straight to her apartment, William decided to take the long way back to the city with a detour along Lake Shore Drive so they could enjoy the grandeur of the city lights as they talked about their future together. Neither wanted a long engagement nor a particularly big wedding, so perhaps the greatest challenge would be informing the Bennets on New Year's Day of their plans.

William didn't leave Elizabeth's apartment until they had watched the sunrise together and greeted the day as a newly engaged couple. Even though they had little sleep to sustain them, the happy pair arrived at the Bennet residence promptly at one in the afternoon. There, a full day of football, good food and happy fellowship awaited them.

"How long do you think it will take our sisters to notice your ring?" William asked as they traversed the walkway to the Bennets' front door.

"I'd say no more than thirty seconds once I take off my coat and gloves. "Sisters are very observant about that kind of thing, you know."

"Not really, but I guess I'm about to find out."

"It's my mother you really have to worry about. She probably will be speechless for a full minute or so and then she'll head straight for the cooking sherry to calm her nerves. You might want to hang out with my dad for a while and avoid her *exuberance* once the reality of our engagement actually takes hold."

"I'll definitely keep that bit of advice in mind." He smiled.

~ ♪ ~

"Hey, everyone, Lizzy and William are here!" Lydia called out when the happy couple walked through the front door and began taking off their coats.

"William," Georgie called hurrying over and giving him and Elizabeth each a hug. "Wait until you see how much food we've cooked. You'll never believe it. The Bennets have *two* refrigerators, and they are both full!"

All at once Lydia grabbed Georgiana's arm and started screaming, "Georgie, Kitty! Oh, my gosh, my gosh! Lizzy and William are engaged!"

Before William and Elizabeth even made it out of the foyer, the volume in the house suddenly went up dramatically. The sisters all crowded around Elizabeth, asking a multitude of question simultaneously while admiring her engagement ring. As predicted, Mrs. Bennet headed straight for the kitchen cupboard and poured herself an ample glass of her favorite sherry. Mr. Bennet came into the front room to see what all the commotion was about. After shaking William's hand and welcoming him into the family, he kissed Elizabeth on the cheek and then conveniently retreated back to the television room, lest he miss any of the important pre-game highlights for the day.

Emerging from the kitchen, Mrs. Bennet finally found her voice and exclaimed, "Elizabeth Bennet! You are going to be the death of me!" Everyone had a good laugh, and Elizabeth gave a very abridged overview of their evening at the Country Club and how William had romantically proposed to her at midnight. Georgie was beside herself knowing she was going to have a new sister and would be an official part of the Bennet family from now on. During the next hour, the Gardiners, Mary, and Jane and Charles arrived, prompting the fuss to begin all over again.

CHAPTER 9

BE MY LOVE

Briar Ridge Country Club
14 February

"Lizzy," called Lydia as she, Kitty and Georgiana hurried into the anteroom where Elizabeth, Jane and Mary were almost finished getting dressed. "Mom says everything is ready to go in the ballroom, and she'll be here as soon as she has a few last words with the minister. You should see all the guests! This place is packed, and here I thought you said it would be a small wedding."

"Very funny, Lydia! With our mother being the ultimate wedding planner, it's amazing we were able to keep the guest list down to two hundred. Believe it or not, William and I were sure we would have a *small, intimate wedding* when we only gave Mom a month's notice to plan everything." The girls chuckled knowing Mrs. Bennet's propensity for planning a party. She and her friends from the woman's circle had been working around the clock making preparations for Elizabeth and William's special day. After all, Elizabeth was the first daughter to get married in the Bennet family and Franny was determined to make it the wedding of every woman's dreams.

"Georgie, did you see William? I was wondering how he's holding up out there."

"My brother always puts on a good face, but secretly, I think he's probably more nervous than you are. He must have been up half the night pacing around the condo. Even *I* had trouble sleeping with all of the racket he was making."

"Well, let's hope he'll start to relax once we get through the ceremony. By the way, the music from the string quartet sounds wonderful. The kids are doing a great job. I only wish I was in the hall listening instead of fussing over how I look. I can hardly wait to hear what the Vocalteens have planned for the reception."

Rising from the dressing table, Elizabeth turned and faced her newest sister. "What do you think, Georgie? Will William like the way I look?" Elizabeth had on an A-line skirt, empire waist, sheer back, sleeveless dress with floor-length flowing chiffon and French lace applique on the bodice. Her hair was pulled up on the sides and a mass of chocolate curls trailed down her back.

"Oh, Lizzy," Georgiana gushed. "You look like a princess!"

"Not quite." She beamed. "I still need help with your mother's pearls." William and Georgiana had presented Elizabeth with the same pearl necklace and earrings that Anne Darcy wore when she married their father, James.

Georgiana had tears in her eyes as Elizabeth held her hair to the side so she could fasten the clasp at the back of her neck. "Lizzy, my mother would have loved you, and I'm so glad you are wearing these in her honor."

Elizabeth turned around and hugged Georgiana before gently wiping her moist cheeks. "These pearls are very precious, and I promise to take good care of them. Someday *you* will wear them at *your* wedding." Again they hugged.

Moments later, Mrs. Bennet came bustling through the door intent on taking one final look at all of the girls. "Beautiful, beautiful," she repeated over and over until she finally stood in front of Elizabeth. "Absolutely stunning!" she said in praise of her second eldest.

"The pearls are exquisite, my dear. Between my lace handkerchief, the pearls and your dress, we have covered something old, new and borrowed. All that remains is to give you these." Mrs. Bennet proudly held up a blue garter and a silver sixpence causing everyone to laugh as she said, "I'm not taking any chances." [1]

Jane helped Elizabeth with the added accessories while Mrs. Bennet said her last piece. "Well, Lizzy, despite you trying my poor nerves for the past month, everything is ready, and your young man is anxiously waiting for you to walk down the aisle with your father. I'm very proud of you."

"Thanks, Mom. You have no idea how much William and I appreciate all of the work you and the circle ladies have done to make our day so special. I love you." She kissed her mother on the cheek causing Mrs. Bennet to tear up.

"I love you too, Lizzy." Mrs. Bennet nervously patted her chest in an effort to control her emotions. Taking a deep breath she was finally able to say, "Girls, I believe it is time for all of you to take your places." The bridesmaids gave their sister one last hug and then proceeded to the ballroom where Elizabeth Anne Bennet and William James Darcy were joined as man and wife on Valentine's Day, one of the most romantic holidays of the year.

The reception

In everyone's mind, there could not have been a more beautiful wedding. Forest Ridge Country Club was an ideal setting, and as it was mid-week, William had no problems securing the facility on such short notice. Rising to the occasion, Mrs. Bennet's efforts went far beyond what anyone might have anticipated. From the decorations to the caterers, everything was well thought-out and beautifully executed. The heartfelt music sung by the academy students was touching and Skip Evans' trio only added to the romantic atmosphere already pervading the hall during the reception.

By the time all of the well-wishers had said their piece and made their toasts, the happy couple was more than ready to have a few moments alone on the dance floor. "Mrs. Darcy," William addressed Elizabeth as he led her through a turn and pulled her close to his chest. "Have I told you how lovely you look tonight and how very much I love you?" He tenderly caressed her cheek with his fingertips before placing a soft kiss on her lips.

"Yes, Mr. Darcy," she answered rather dreamy-eyed. "I love you too, but I wouldn't mind if you told me again."

"My darling girl," he whispered into her hair. "I love you with every breath of my being, and I intend to show just how much for the rest of our lives, starting with tonight."

"William," she momentarily blushed knowing what he was referring to. "Does this mean I can convince you to tell me where you're taking me for our honeymoon?" Her teasing smile was bewitching.

"Liz, when you smile at me like that, how can I resist?" He kissed the back of her hand. "Following the reception, the limo will take us to our honeymoon suite, and then at ten in the morning, we board a plane for Hawaii."

"Hawaii?" Her eyes grew wide with the thought.

"Yes, my love. For eight days and nights I shall have you all to myself. There will be no sisters, no extended family members, no co-workers or students—just you and me in a tropical paradise, *alone*."

"*Alone*," she mouthed as she touched his face and leaned in for another kiss. "Will, you are going to spoil me."

"That's my intention, sweetheart."

"My present for you is not nearly as grand." She shyly smiled.

"You have something for me?"

"I do. If you don't mind, I asked Skip if we could revive our duet from Bingley's party."

"I would like nothing better, Liz."

With that Elizabeth took William by the hand and led him over to where the trio was playing. Taking the mic in one hand, she lovingly said, "William Darcy, this song is for you."

When I fall in love

*It will be forever
And the moment
I can feel that you feel that way too
Is when I fall in love
With you.*

When I Fall in Love – by Victor Young and Edward Heyman

EPILOGUE

A little more than a year later the Darcys were well settled into their new residence in the famed Frank Lloyd District of Meryton Heights. Both William and Elizabeth loved historical architecture and didn't hesitate to put in a bid on the old house when they first saw it. The house was only a short distance from the academy, which worked out perfectly for the girls, and William could easily catch a train into the city for meetings when he wasn't working from home.

As one might imagine, holidays still played a very important part in the lives of the newly married couple. May twelfth, Mother's Day, proved to be no exception. When the day finally arrived, Master William James Darcy II made his voice known to the world after testing his parents with thirteen hours of labor. The proud parents couldn't be happier with their long and lean healthy boy who possessed an abundance of silky dark curls.

A few hours after having informed the family of their joyous news, William happily sat down on the bed where Elizabeth and his son were resting. "Liz, I love you and little Will so much," he said, lovingly kissing his wife on the forehead. He was in awe as he watched their hungry child suckling at her breast, a precious vision he would never forget.

Elizabeth stroked the babe's soft curls and looked up at her husband saying, "I love you, too, William. He's so perfect." She smiled with tears glistening in her eyes. "You know, of all the holidays we've shared together, this one is now my favorite."

"Mine too, sweetheart." He wiped her moist cheek with his finger. Moments later, he reached for his son's hand, allowing the little fingers to wrap around one of his own. "*A Holiday to Remember.*" They smiled at one another and kissed knowing this was the way things were meant to be. Their lives would be filled with countless holidays and treasured memories which would continue to bless their days with joy and love.

~ Finis ~

TWELVE DAYS ~ A REGENCY SHORT STORY

Day 1

Darcy House
The breakfast room
25 December, 1811

Sitting in his favourite chair, Fitzwilliam Darcy quietly browsed through the paper while sipping his morning coffee. The touch of his wife's hand on his shoulder interrupted his perusal, and he glanced up, appreciating the mischievous sparkle in her eyes, along with the musical sound of her laughter.

Quickly rising and taking Elizabeth into his arms, he kissed her and asked, "To what do I owe the honour of your teasing ways, my love?"

"Teasing?" She arched a brow in his direction. "I could ask the same of you, my dear husband. Instead I shall simply express gratitude for my very *unusual* present."

"Unusual present? Elizabeth, I am sure I do not understand your meaning."

"Why, I am referring to *a partridge in a pear tree* now residing in the solarium," she giggled. "Do you intend to shower me with *all* of the gifts which are mentioned in that old yule rhyme?[1] If such is the case, I fear we shall have an excess of birds, and Cook will not be happy."

"Elizabeth, there must be some mistake," he puzzled. "Though I would have no problem showering you with gifts for twelve days, I assure you I did *not* send *a partridge in a pear tree*. Was there no message?"

"No, husband, there was not. I naturally assumed it was from you. Shall we go and take a closer look?"

"With pleasure," he offered his arm. "I wonder if this is some trick of Richard's. As a youth, he was known for such pranks." Darcy continued to elaborate on the merits of his cousin's mischief while accompanying his wife to the solarium. Entering the room, they were greeted by the screeching cries of the partridge being chased by a footman.

"Walters, what is going on here?"

"Forgive me, Mr. Darcy," the footman responded while trying to regain his composure. "I was standing watch as Mrs. Darcy instructed when all at once the bird came down from his perch and started fluttering to and fro. I tried to catch him with the intention of restraining him in this box, but to no avail. As you can see, the bird has begun to create a mess with his droppings and has damaged some of the leaves on the potted plants."

While Walters was speaking, Elizabeth had her own idea of what to do. Moving to a corner table, she quickly removed the items resting on top in order to free the tablecloth.

"Mr. Walters, please try using this cloth to subdue the bird." Five minutes later, the task was accomplished.

"I shall take this bird to Cook at once." Walters bowed and quickly left.

"Elizabeth." Darcy was not happy. "I believe it is time to send Richard a note."

Day 2

The study
26 December, 1811

Darcy was busy sorting through his mail when his wife stepped into the room. "Fitzwilliam." She smiled radiantly and hurried to his desk where he took her by the hand and pulled her onto his lap for a lingering kiss.

"You are very happy today. Is there something I should know, my love?" He questioned.

"Another present has arrived, and I thought I would try to soften you before breaking the news."

"Oh?" He scowled. "I suppose it is the *two turtle doves*."

"Yes." She bit her lip before continuing. "And … there is another *partridge in a pear tree*."

"What!" He bellowed. Removing his wife from his lap, Darcy rose and began to pace the floor in agitation. "Elizabeth, I shall not stand for this. Richard has gone too far this time. I tell you, I refuse to have our house filled with trees and birds. This nonsense must stop!"

"I agree, but if it is any consolation, Georgiana thinks that the *two turtle doves* are very pretty and would be happy to keep them as pets."

"Humph! Richard must have received my message by now." Darcy pinched the bridge of his nose hoping to stave off a headache. "I shall send him another note, and if he does not respond today, I will have no choice but to go to Matlock House on the morrow and confront him in person."

Elizabeth quickly moved in front of her husband in an effort to stop his pacing. Grabbing his hands and putting them around her waist, she smiled and pulled his face down to hers for another kiss. "Fitzwilliam, I am determined not to let your mood spoil our day. Walters has taken care of the new partridge, and we shall deal with the tree later. May we not take a long walk this morning? It is a lovely winter day, and I am sure the fresh air will make you feel better."

"Forgive me." He kissed her again. "A long walk followed by some time alone with you in our chambers would be very much to my liking."

"Then let us leave at once."

<h1 style="text-align:center">Day 3</h1>

Matlock House
27 December, 1811

"Darcy, what brings you here today?" Colonel Fitzwilliam's voice was husky and barely audible. "Sorry if I seem to be under the weather."

"Richard, you look terrible. I was about to ask why you have ignored my messages, but now I can see for myself. Should you not be in bed?"

Taking out a handkerchief, he sneezed before complaining, "Devil of a cold. Sorry, I have yet to read my mail. Tell me, in my limited capacity, how may I be of service today?"

"Actually, I came here to accuse you of a prank, but now I am not so sure."

"A prank?"

"Yes, for three days, Darcy House has been besieged by unusual gifts. It all started on the twenty-fifth with *a partridge in a pear tree*. I must admit the bird was very tasty and Cook did make splendid pear butter, but that is hardly the point. Yesterday, we were gifted with *two turtle doves* AND another *partridge in a pear tree*. Finally today, the *three French hens* were delivered in addition to two more *turtle doves* and..."

"Let me guess, *a partridge in a pear tree*."

"Just so!"

Colonel Fitzwilliam laughed so hard that he broke into a fit of coughing. "Priceless!" he barely choked out. "I am sorry to say it was not me who sent the gifts. I only wish I had the resources to be so creative."

"Richard!" He glared. "More importantly, the question becomes how do I stop these *gifts* from coming? Tomorrow's offerings will most likely be the *four colly birds*, and you know what a noisy lot they are. Can you imagine what kind of chaos will prevail at Darcy House if this continues on for twelve days?"

Trying not to cough, the colonel teased, "I cannot help but wonder where you will put the *six geese-a-laying,* as well as the *seven swans-a-swimming.* Your aviary will never house all of those birds and the pond area is hardly adequate. Too bad you are not at Pemberley. At least there you could pass on some of the gifts to your tenants."

"Please!" Frustrated, Darcy raked his hand through his hair and continued. "I am at a loss here. I have no idea if I should enlist the aid of the Bow Street Runners to find the source of these deliveries, or if I should resort to having my footmen stand porter outside my house. What do you suggest I do?"

"I get your point. Although I am not feeling my best, I still have a meeting scheduled with one of my aides later this afternoon. Let me see what I can do."

Day 6

The Club
31 December, 1811

Darcy could hardly believe the attention he garnered as he walked into Whites. Strange sounds like clucking chickens and cawing birds could be heard beneath the din of quiet laughter while patrons bowed with exaggeration or winked in fun. Was there no person who had not heard of his dilemma or had not read about it in the gossip papers? Walking into the lounge, Darcy spotted his cousin sitting at a small table with another gentleman.

Rising, the colonel said, "Mr. Fitzwilliam Darcy, please allow me to introduce Mr. Morris, the investigator I hired on your behalf." Greetings were exchanged, and Darcy took a seat.

Morris appeared nervous as he spoke, his voice high-pitched. "Thus far, I have had difficulty tracing the monetary transactions for your gifts any further than the various establishments where they were purchased. In the case of the *partridges* and the *pear trees,* the proprietor indicated that an elderly gentleman placed the order on behalf of a client who preferred to remain anonymous. I also discovered that more than one shop was contracted in the acquisition of the *French hens* and the *colly birds*. As for the *five gold rings,* a collection of eight sets were ordered by a woman. I regret to say, your benefactor has been rather clever."

"You said eight sets of *gold rings*, Mr. Morris?" Darcy's voice began to rise in agitation.

"That is correct." He winced.

"I care not what it takes. This has to stop. Hire additional investigators, if you must. As of today, I have received a total of six *partridges* and six *pear trees,* ten *turtle doves,* one of which bit my sister's finger, *twelve French hens, twelve colly birds,* two sets of *five gold rings* and this morning, *six geese-a-laying*. The way these gifts are compounding, my property is abounding with fowl, and we are only half way through the twelve days!"

"Darcy, calm down." The colonel grabbed his cousin by the arm as he spoke. "Even if we cannot stop the gifts for the time being, Mother has offered to take the birds so that they may be donated to one of her charities. There are many who are in need of food in the worst part of the city, and she will be sending over several footmen to collect them for distribution. Rest assured, we shall put an end to this madness."

"Humph!"

Day 10

Darcy House
The Study
4 January, 1812

"Elizabeth, please come in. I have had another note from Richard. Apparently, *the nine ladies dancing* who were sent yesterday and today's *ten Lords-a-leaping,* are hired performers who have been without regular employment since the fire at Drury Lane. Richard assures me, for a small fee, the actors will gladly resign their positions and not return for the remaining two days of their performance. It is also my understanding that Mr. Morris has finally put an end to the birds."

"Thank goodness, but does he know anything about the *eleven pipers piping* or the *twelve drummers drumming?*"

"That, my lovely wife, remains to be seen. I am hoping Morris will be able to locate the musicians and stop them from coming here as well. Each day our street has become more crowded with spectators who wish to laugh at our expense. I tell you, Elizabeth, if it was not for my aunt's ball on *Twelfth Night*, I would gladly whisk you away to Pemberley this very day." Darcy reached for his wife, pulled her into his embrace, and kissed the top of her head.

"Fitzwilliam, it still puzzles me as to why anyone would go to all of this trouble and expense to try to embarrass us in this fashion."

"Those, too, are my thoughts. It makes no sense."

"Then again," she playfully teased while trying to wiggle free, "perhaps you have a former lover who is disgruntled over our marriage. Tell me, Mr. Darcy, could that be the problem?"

"I think *not,* my dear." He held her firm and kissed her soundly on the lips. "Rest assured, Elizabeth, you are my first and only love. In truth, Mr. Morris believes this entire fiasco is the work of two people. To be precise, they are a man and a woman who have donned several disguises."

"*Two* people?"

"Yes. Hopefully, they will be caught in the end." He sighed. "Next year, do let us stay in the country for the holidays. I am weary of Town."

Elizabeth reached up and touched her husband's face. "With pleasure, my love."

Several Days Later

"Miss Bingley, the gentleman and lady you were expecting have arrived. Would you care to see them now?"

"Yes, Forsett, please show them in." Caroline quickly folded up the missive she had been reading from her brother's solicitor and put it to the side. Before leaving on holiday with his wife, Charles had authorized Mr. Knox to release additional monies for her use during the holiday season. After all she would need to make purchases for Boxing Day, gifts for a few relatives and certainly some new winter necessities for herself. For some extra coin, the solicitor had turned his head the other way when Caroline presented him with her unusual list of purchases. This particular letter was confirmation that all of her bills had been paid in full.

Picking up a folded copy of the latest gossip paper, she greeted her guests. "I was just enjoying a bit of *tattle* about Mr. and Mrs. Fitzwilliam Darcy. It seems they were besieged with unusual gifts during the holiday season."

"So we have heard," the gentleman purposely nodded to his companion.

"Perhaps you would care to read it for yourself," Caroline drawled, handing the man the publication. The man grinned as he eagerly took the paper and opened it to make sure that what he came for was between the pages.

"Ah, yes, I believe I shall enjoy this article very much," he answered, tucking the paper and monetary contents in his breast pocket.

"Be sure that you do. Should I have need of your services in the future, where may I contact you?"

"Younge's boarding house—Prusom Street, on the east side of Town." The man then tipped his hat, the lady curtsied, and the two of them left as quickly as they had come.

~ Finis ~

OTHER BOOKS BY JENNIFER REDLARCZYK

Darcy's Melody ~ Preview

Inspired by Jane Austen's Pride and Prejudice comes "Darcy's Melody." In the year 1811 the war with France continues to rage, sending many injured men home to England where accommodations are limited. Raising funds to build an additional structure at the London Hospital for the wounded has become a top priority for Lady Eleanor Fitzwilliam, Countess of Matlock. She has not only enlisted members of the *ton* to assist with her committee, but women who are well-known throughout the trade community. It is within this endeavour that Elizabeth Bennet and Georgiana Darcy meet through a mutual love of music. This is the story of how music and friendship bring two families together, challenging Fitzwilliam Darcy to embrace a new melody within his heart.

FROM CHAPTER ONE

London
Tuesday, 21 May 1811
Early afternoon

Ballard's was an eclectic treasure trove of rare first editions and unusual books located on the thoroughfare of Piccadilly. Although it appeared somewhat dingy and dimly lit from the outside, inside the ageing building the atmosphere was inviting, and a vast array of literature beckoned lovers of the written word.

Promptly at one o'clock, Fitzwilliam Darcy entered the bookshop and walked directly towards his favoured section. While paging through a military war journal, he instinctively glanced toward the back of the shop. Even with several patrons milling about the establishment today, Darcy's eyes were drawn to a young lady who appeared to be examining a small book in the poetry section.

Closing the journal, Darcy ambled over to where the woman stood and began perusing the titles on a nearby shelf. After taking a book in hand, he purposely turned his head towards the young lady. Captivated by her large, dark emerald-green eyes sparkling with mischief, he felt his lips curve into a half smile when she spoke.

"Pray, sir, may I trouble you to hand me the book of Cowper poetry on the upper shelf?"

Darcy nodded. "With pleasure. Cowper is an excellent choice."

As he reached for the book, she continued, "One poem in particular reminds me of Oakham Mount in *Hertfordshire*. I find I am rather desirous of its solace today if only through the eyes of the poet."

Handing her the book, he answered in kind. "I understand your sentiments for I, too, am from the country and have longed to return to *Derbyshire*."

Arching an eyebrow in his direction, she inclined her head and said, "I thank you, sir."

"You are most welcome."

As she turned the pages of her selection in search of the poem, Darcy heard the young lady gasp when both of her books slid out of her hands and onto the floor. "Oh dear," she sighed, stooping down to retrieve them.

"Allow me," he immediately offered. Both reaching for the books, Darcy felt her small, warm hand carefully slip a folded piece of paper into the palm of his own. The young lady had not replaced her glove after perusing her own book, and her skin was soft to the touch. Leaning closer, the faint scent of lavender seemed to strengthen, causing his chest to tighten and his heart to quicken in response.

Feigning innocence, she looked up at him and said, "Again, sir, I am in your debt. Perhaps I should make my purchases before I have another mishap."

"Permit me to carry these to the desk for you."

Acknowledging his offer with a slight curtsey, the young lady whispered, "Sir, I think we are being observed." Then speaking louder, she added, "Thank you again. You are most kind."

"Your servant." He bowed. With his senses heightened from being forewarned of impending danger, Darcy spoke softly in return, "How did you come? I would not have you leave here unescorted."

"There is a carriage waiting, sir. A manservant is nearby and a maid is within."

"Then leave now and be careful."

After he placed the books on the counter, the young lady thanked Darcy, made her purchase, and quickly exited the shop. From where he stood, Darcy watched the footman assist her into the carriage. Assured of her safety, he abruptly turned and faced the observing patron who had folded his newspaper and was preparing to leave the shop.

"Excuse me, have we met?"

The man was obviously confused and stammered, "I ... I think so. You are Mr. erm.... "

"Fitzwilliam Darcy. And you are?"

"My name is ... is Gerard Mooreland, and if I remember correctly, my son, Jonathan, was a classmate of yours at university some years back."

Darcy furrowed his brow for a moment in thought. "I do not seem to recall the name. Do you care to refresh my memory?"

"My ... my son was a master with the blade and was an active participant in the fencing club," Mooreland boasted through a somewhat crooked smile.

With no recollection of either man, Darcy made further inquiries after which he gave Mooreland his card and requested his son pay him a visit when he was next in Town. Concluding their conversation, Darcy made his purchase and left the bookshop being rather unsettled.

DARCY'S MELODY

A VERY MERRY MIX-UP ~ PREVIEW

It all began when Fitzwilliam Darcy and his cousin Colonel Richard Fitzwilliam stopped at the posting station in Bromley on their way to Rosings Park for their annual visit. Looking for some diversion, the good colonel happened upon a local Romani woman who was selling her people's treasured *Moon Wine*. Find out what happens to some of our favourite Jane Austen characters when her advice is ignored in *A Very Merry Mix-up*.

FROM CHAPTER ONE

1 April 1811
All Fool's Day
Kent

Fitzwilliam Darcy yawned and stretched, squinting as the early morning light flickered through the partially opened curtains of his bedroom window. For some unknown reason, he had not slept well. Bleary-eyed and wondering if the potent wine he had drunk on the previous evening had been the cause, he slowly rolled over intending to stay in bed a bit longer. To his chagrin, his senses were alerted when his hand met with the soft, warm body of a woman.

"Good God! Who are you?" he bellowed, startling the woman who was sharing his bed.

The woman's breath nearly caught in her throat when she turned over and saw who was by her side. "WHAT, may I ask, are YOU doing in MY bed?" Quickly pulling the sheets up to her neckline, she continued. "I demand you leave THIS INSTANT!"

"You are.... You are Mrs. Collins!" he shouted in distress.

"Mrs. Collins!" she shouted back. "Sir, you are mad! I am your cousin, Elizabeth Bennet, and I DO believe my dear friend Charlotte will NOT be happy when I tell her of your indiscretion."

"MY indiscretion?! Madam, you are in MY bed!"

Quickly rising, Darcy felt a little unsteady and found it necessary to hold on to the bed post while searching for his robe. Catching a glimpse of himself in the mirror, he staggered closer to the glass and groaned in disbelief. Slowly rubbing his stubby fingers across his ruddy cheeks and through his oily hair, he wondered if he had indeed gone mad. Wiping those same fingers on the front of his nightshirt, he could not help but feel his flabby chest and the protrusion of his round stomach through the cloth. Grasping the reality of his predicament, Darcy stared at himself with revulsion.

"Merciful Heaven!" he thundered, turning back to the woman. "It is me, Fitzwilliam Darcy, in the body of that idiot rector! If you are Miss Elizabeth Bennet, as you claim, I fear we have both become the victims of some cruel joke. Will you not come and look for yourself?"

Picking up Charlotte's dressing gown and quickly wrapping it around herself, Elizabeth guardedly went to the mirror as he requested. "Mr. Darcy?" She paled, realizing what he said was true. "How ... how could this have happened?"

"I do not know," he said momentarily pinching his brow in hope of staving off a sudden headache. "But ... I have a feeling Colonel Fitzwilliam may have some answers. I suspect *this misfortune* has something to do with the wine which he offered us following dinner."

"The wine?"

"Yes," he nearly hissed. "Did you not feel a little strange after drinking it?"

"I did, but I thought it was nothing more than the warmth of the room created by the burning logs which were piled high for Miss de Bourgh's comfort."

"At the time, my thoughts were the same as yours." He scowled. "In retrospect, I am more inclined to believe it was *not* the heat, but rather the wine which we consumed. The *good colonel* insisted on buying that particular bottle from an old woman who was selling it out of the posting station at Bromley on our journey here. While I have never been one to embrace superstitions, in this instance perhaps I should have paid more attention. I vaguely remember overhearing the woman cautioning my cousin when it came to drinking the wine and making wishes during a full moon."

"Oh, dear," Elizabeth murmured more to herself than to Darcy. "Yesterday evening, the moon *was* full, and the last thing I remember was wishing I could see you…." Gasping, she took a step back not wanting to say more.

"What!" he demanded.

"Forgive me." She tried to remain calm. "You are always so fastidious in your appearance, Mr. Darcy. I … I merely wondered what it would be like to see you in … in a more unkempt state. I promise you, I would never wish to see any man exchange places with Mr. Collins. That would be too cruel, indeed. Pray, sir, did you not make a wish of your own to have ended up in this predicament with me?" Her eyes suddenly grew wide realizing the truth of what Mr. Darcy's stares must have meant all along. *It must have been admiration and not simply to find fault.*

Clearing his throat, Darcy stated, "It matters not what I wished for, Madam. More importantly, we need to find out who else was affected by the wine and what course of action can be taken to rectify this dilemma."

"Yes, of course." Her face coloured. "Mr. Darcy, you will find Mr. Collins' room through the door just behind you. It would be best if you took your leave now. I should like to dress and find out if Charlotte has taken my place."

"I beg your pardon. Forgive me, I was not thinking. I should not be here and shall leave you at once." His face reddened at the impropriety of his appearance and the situation he found himself in.

"I shall await your arrival downstairs. For now, it would be best if we do nothing to alert the servants of the changes which have taken place. Meanwhile, I shall send a note to my cousin asking him to come directly." Darcy abruptly left the room feeling very unsettled.

A VERY MERRY MIX-UP

PEMBERLEY'S TREASURES: A collection of short stories inspired by Jane Austen's Pride and Prejudice will be published in August of 2019.

ABOUT THE AUTHOR

JENNIFER REDLARCZYK

I am a private music instructor living in Crown Point, Indiana where I teach voice, violin and piano and work as an adjunct music professor at Purdue University Northwest in Hammond, Indiana. As a teen, I was introduced to Jane Austen by my mother who loved old books, old movies and old songs. In the summer of 2011, I stumbled upon Jane Austen Fanfiction at a local book store and became a loyal fan of this genre. Since then, I met several talented JAFF authors and devoted readers who were active on social media and eventually became a moderator for the private JAFF forum, DarcyandLizzy.com. It was there that I first tried my hand at writing short stories. I have the greatest appreciation for the creative world of Jane Austen Fanfiction and am thrilled to be a part of the JAFF community. You can find me at: DarcyandLizzy.com, Facebook, Twitter, Pinterest, and YouTube. On my Pinterest page you will find inspiration pictures for each chapter of *A Holiday to Remember* as well as my other books. ~ Jennifer Redlarczyk (Jen Red) ~ ♫ ~

NOTES

CHAPTER 1

1. Lollapalooza is an annual music festival in Chicago featuring popular alternative rock, heavy metal, punk rock, hip hop, and electronic music bands and artists, dance and comedy performances, and craft booths.
2. Latin School of Chicago is a selective private elementary, middle, and high school located in the Gold Coast neighborhood on the near north side of Chicago. The school was founded in 1888 and is the oldest independent day school in the city.
3. Ketamine, a popular date-rape drug, is legal in the United States for use as an anesthetic for humans and animals. Veterinary clinics are often robbed for their ketamine supplies.

CHAPTER 9

1. "Something old" is the first line of a traditional rhyme dated from 1883. It details what a bride should wear at the wedding for good luck: Something old, something new, something borrowed something blue, and a silver sixpence in her shoe.

TWELVE DAYS ~ A REGENCY SHORT STORY

1. The best known version of "The Twelve Days of Christmas" was first printed in English in 1780 without music and was recited as a chant or rhyme. It appeared in a little book for children called, *Mirth without Mischief,* as a Twelfth Night *memories-and-forfeits* game. The standard tune now associated with this poem, is derived from a 1909 arrangement by English composer Frederic Austin. There are twelve cumulative verses, each describing a gift given by "my true love," starting on December 25th. The gifts not only have a playful meaning but symbolize religious events pertaining to the life of Christ.

Made in the USA
Middletown, DE
22 March 2019